NEW YORK REVIEW BOOKS
CLASSICS

FAT CITY

LEONARD GARDNER was born in Stockton, California. His short stories and articles have appeared in *The Paris Review*, *Esquire*, *Southwest Review*, and *Brick*, among other magazines. His screen adaptation of *Fat City* was made into a film by John Huston in 1972; he subsequently worked as a writer for independent film and television. For his work on the series *NYPD Blue* he twice received a Humanitas Prize (1997 and 1999) as well as a Peabody Award (1998). In 2008 he was the recipient of the A. J. Liebling Award, given by the Boxing Writers Association of America. A former Guggenheim Fellow, he lives in Northern California.

DENIS JOHNSON has published eight novels as well as novellas, short stories, reportage, poetry, and plays. His novel *Tree of Smoke* won the 2007 National Book Award.

T0018485

FAT CITY

LEONARD GARDNER

Introduction by
DENIS JOHNSON

NEW YORK REVIEW BOOKS

New York

THIS IS A NEW YORK REVIEW BOOK
PUBLISHED BY THE NEW YORK REVIEW OF BOOKS
207 East 32nd Street, New York, NY 10016
www.nyrb.com

Library of Congress Cataloging-in-Publication Data
Gardner, Leonard.
  Fat city / by Leonard Gardner ; introduction by Denis Johnson.
    pages ; cm. — (New York Review Books classics)
  ISBN 978-1-59017-892-8 (alk. paper)
  1. Boxers (Sports)—Fiction. 2. Young men—Fiction. 3. Stockton (Calif.)—
Fiction. 4. Sports stories. I. Title.
  PS3557.A713F3 2015
  813'.54—dc23

                              2015019900

ISBN 978-1-59017-892-8
Available as an electronic book; ISBN 978-1-59017-893-5

Printed in the United States of America on acid-free paper.
10 9 8 7 6 5

INTRODUCTION

Exactly which year of the 1960s the book came out, I can't remember, but I remember well which year of my lifetime it was—I was discovering that it wasn't a joke anymore, I was actually going to have to become a writer, I was too emotionally crippled for real work, there wasn't anything else I could do—I was eighteen or nineteen. *Newsweek* reviewed *Fat City*, a first novel by Leonard Gardner, in a tone that seemed to drop the usual hype—"It's good. It really is." I wanted to get a review like that.

I got the book and read about two Stockton, California, boxers who live far outside the boxing myth and deep in the sorrow and beauty of human life, a book so precisely written and giving such value to its words that I felt I could almost read it with my fingers, like Braille.

The stories of Ernie Munger, a young fighter with frail but nevertheless burning hopes, and Billy Tully, an older pug with bad luck in and out of the ring, parallel one another through the book. Though the two men hardly meet, the tale blends the perspective on them until they seem to chart a single life of missteps and baffled love, Ernie its youth and Tully its future. I wanted to write a book like that.

My neighbor across the road, also a young literary hopeful, felt the same. We talked about every paragraph of *Fat City* one by one and over and over, the way couples sometimes reminisce about each moment of their falling in love.

And like most youngsters in the throes, I assumed I was among the very few humans who'd ever felt this way. In the next few years, studying at the Writers' Workshop in Iowa City, I was astonished every time I met a young writer who could quote ecstatically line after line of dialogue from the down-and-out souls of *Fat City*, the men and women seeking love, a bit of comfort, even glory—but never forgiveness—in the heat and dust of central California. Admirers were everywhere.

My friend across the road saw Gardner in a drugstore in California once, recognized him from his jacket photo. He was looking at a boxing magazine. "Are you Leonard Gardner?" my friend asked. "You must be a writer," Gardner said, and went back to the magazine. I made him tell the story a thousand times.

Between the ages of nineteen and twenty-five I studied Leonard Gardner's book so closely that I began to fear I'd never be able to write anything but imitations of it, so I swore it off.

When I was about thirty-four (the same age Gardner was when he published his), my first novel came out. About a year later I borrowed *Fat City* from the library and read it. I could see immediately that ten years' exile hadn't saved me from the influence of its perfection—I'd taught myself to write in Gardner's style, though not as well. And now, many years later, it's still true: Leonard Gardner has something to say in every word I write.

—DENIS JOHNSON

FAT CITY

I

He lived in the Hotel Coma—named perhaps for some
founder of the town, some California explorer or pio-
neer, or for some long-deceased Italian immigrant who
founded only the hotel itself. Whoever it commemo-
rated, the hotel was a poor monument, and Billy Tully
had no intention of staying on. His clean laundry he
continued to put back in his suitcase on the dresser,
ready to be hurried away to better lodgings. He had
lived in five hotels in the year and a half since his wife
had left him. From his window he looked out on the
stunted skyline of Stockton—a city of eighty thousand
surrounded by the sloughs, rivers and fertile fields of
the San Joaquin River delta—a view of business buildings, church spires, chimneys, water towers, gas tanks
and the low roofs of residences rising among leafless
trees between absolutely flat streets. Along the sidewalk under his window, men passed between bars and
liquor stores, cafés, secondhand stores and walk-up hotels. Pigeons the color of the street pecked in the gutters, flew between buildings, marched along ledges and
cooed on Tully's sill. His room was high and narrow.

Smudges from oily heads darkened the wallpaper between the metal rods of his bed. His shade was tattered, his light bulb dim, and his neighbors all seemed to have lung trouble.

Billy Tully was a fry cook in a Main Street lunchroom. His face, a youthful pink, was lined around the mouth. There was a dent in the middle of his nose. Thin scars lay one above another at the outer edges of his brows. Crew-cut on top and combed back long on the sides, his rust-colored hair was abundant. He was short, deep-chested, compact, neither heavy nor thin nor very muscular, his bones thick, his flesh spare. It was the size of his neck that gave his clothed figure its look of strength. The result of years of exercise, of lifting ten- and twenty-pound weights with a headstrap, it had been developed for a single purpose—to absorb the shock of blows.

Tully had not had a bout since his wife had left him, but last night he had hit a man in the Ofis Inn. What the argument involved he could no longer clearly recall, and he gave it little thought. What concerned him was what had been revealed about himself. He had thrown one punch and the man had dropped. Tully now believed he had given up his career too soon. He was still only twenty-nine.

Down stairs carpeted with rubber safety treads, where someone fell nearly every night, he set off for the YMCA to test himself on the punching bags. Enjoying a sense of renewal after a morning of hangover, he walked quickly along the cold streets.

In a subterranean locker room, hearing a din from the swimming pool, Tully removed his clothes. He had four tattoos, obtained while in the army and now utterly disgusting to him: a blue swallow in flight over each nipple, a green snake wound up his left wrist, and on the inside of his right forearm a dagger piercing a rose. Wearing pale-blue trunks and a gray T-shirt, he went silently down a corridor on soft leather soles toward the sound of a furiously punched bag. When Tully entered the room at the end of the corridor, a tall, lean, sweating youth glanced up, took a final swing at the bag and sat down on a bench amid a disarray of barbells on the cracked concrete floor. There was no one else in the room. Tully swung his arms, rolled his neck, squatted, and rose in alarm at a loud pop in his knee, conscious all the while of the boy's stillness. After his violent activity at the bag, he now sat motionless on the bench, looking at the wall. It was the attitude of one wishing to repel attention, and so, perversely, Tully invited him to box, though he himself had come here only to punch the bag.

The boy rose then, quickly and gloomily. "You a pro?"

Tully could see he was looking at his brows. "I was. I'm all out of shape now. We'll just fool around easy, and I can show you a few things, okay? I won't hit you hard."

His face morose, the boy went off to check out the gloves. Tully continued his warm-up and was breathing heavily by the time the other returned. They pulled on the gloves in silence and entered the ring. When Tully reached out to touch gloves, the boy sprang warily away. Smiling tolerantly, Tully pursued him. After that he felt only desperation because everything happened so quickly: smashes on his nose, jolts against his mouth and eyes, the long body eluding him, bounding unbelievably about the ring while Tully, flinching and covering, tried to set himself to counter. In sudden rage he lunged, swinging like a street fighter, and his leg buckled. Hissing with pain, he began hopping around the ring.

That was how it ended. Bent over, kneading a pulled calf muscle, his face contorted, Tully asked between clenched teeth: "What's your name, anyway?"

The boy remained at the far side of the ring. "Ernie Munger."

"How many bouts you had?"

"None."

"You're shitting me. How old are you?"

"Eighteen."

Tully gingerly took a step. "Well, you got it, kid. I fought Fermin Soto, I know what I'm talking about. I mean nobody used to hit me. They couldn't hit me. They'd punch, I wouldn't be there. You ought to start fighting."

"I don't know. I just come down to mess around. Get a little exercise."

"Don't waste your good years. You ought to go over to the Lido Gym and see my manager."

In the showers, Tully was thankful he had not gone to the Lido Gym himself. Beside him water streamed over Ernie Munger's head. The boy's shoulders were broad, his chest flat and hairless, his waist narrow, his arms and legs long and slender, and looking at his face, Tully regretted that he had not had a chance to hit it squarely. It was well formed and callow, the forehead wide and high, the nose prominent. In the dressing room with a towel around his waist, Tully brought a pint of Thunderbird from his athletic bag, and sensitive to its impropriety here in the YMCA, he took a drink with the metal door of his locker blocking him from Ernie's view. In the ceiling a ventilator labored in vain against the odors of sweat and soap and musty athletic clothes.

Tully limped upstairs and, whispering curses at his leg, started back toward his hotel. The sun was setting on a gray day, tinting mauve the flat undersides of clouds beyond the deserted shipyard where two great cranes slanted against the sky. Leaves and papers blew along the gutters. Boats rocked in the floating sheds of the yacht harbor. Farther down the channel a lone freighter was moored by a silo fifty miles from the sea.

There were few figures along Center Street. In the Harbor Inn half the stools were empty. Tully seated himself with care, grasping the edge of the bar. Opposite the notice

> PLEASE DON'T SPIT
> ON THE FLOOR
> GET UP AND SPIT
> IN THE TOILET BOWL
> I thank you

he ate a pickled pig's foot on a napkin and drank a glass of port. He was eating a bag of pork cracklings when a familiar couple sat beside him. The man was a Negro, with a parted mustache and bald temples, his face indolent and dejected. The woman was white, near Tully's age, with thin pencil lines where her eyebrows had been and a broken nose much like his own.

"Don't you ever go home?" she asked him.

"I just got here."

She turned to her companion. "What's keeping him? He knows we're here. Can't you make him come over and serve us?"

"Just take it easy. He be here."

"Well, you spineless son-of-a-bitch, you'd take up for anybody against me." She stared ahead, face propped in both hands. "I want a cream sherry." Then she was again speaking to Tully. "Earl and I have something very wonderful together. I love that man more than any man's got a right to be loved. I couldn't live without him. If he left me I just couldn't make it. But you think he'd even raise his voice to get me a drink? No. He'll just sit there and let him ignore us."

"Here he come," said Earl.

"No thanks to you."

Tully shifted his leg, wincing. He gave a small groan and the woman glanced at him. "Charley horse," he said. When she did not inquire, he went on to tell what had happened to him just as he had been about to get into shape.

She spoke over her shoulder. "Earl?"

"Uh huh."

"This guy's a fighter."

"Oh yeah?"

"Christ. Why did I even mention it? What do you know about it anyway?"

"Not much."

"That's what I mean. Sorry to bother you. Why did

I open my mouth? I apologize. Well, what do you want? I said I was sorry, what more can I say?"

Earl gazed toward the mirror, where a row of gloomy faces looked out into the room. "I hear you, baby."

"You sure don't act like it." With a sigh she took up her glass. "Sometimes I wonder why I put up with him. Basically they're a mistrustful people. You don't know the things I do for that man, but he couldn't care less. You're not as black as he is, then you're shit in his book. He don't like me talking to you, I know. I got to talk to *some*body."

"This kid could make a lot of money some day," Tully continued. "He's a natural athlete."

"What's his name?" Earl inquired, leaning in front of the woman, his face impassive.

"You wouldn't know who he was if he did tell you."

"Just asking."

"Got to know everything. Now he won't talk. He's mad. Butts in and then shuts up. I wanted to hear this."

"There's nothing more to hear. That's it. The kid's a natural, that's all. They come along about one in a million." Enjoying himself, Tully signaled for another drink.

"He's so goddamn sour. I'm having a good talk, that's what's eating him. I don't see why I can't have a little fun. Let him sit there and stew, I don't care. If that's what he wants, why should I? I believe everybody's got a right to live his own life. So screw everybody." She straightened, her voice louder. "I want to say something. I want to give a toast to this gentleman. I'll make it short, just a few words. Here's to your health. God bless you and keep you in all your battles."

Not a head turned as she raised her glass. With large, dark, intense eyes she regarded Tully until he too, in embarrassment and sudden erotic curiosity, lifted his drink.

"Oma?"

"What is it?"

"Nothing."

She turned. "For Christ's sake, what do you want then? Can't I even talk to anybody?"

"I'm not stopping you."

"No, you're not stopping me. Oh, no, you just sit there with your sad-ass face shut until the minute I start having a good time. I'm sick of your bellyaching. Is it my fault if you can't fit in? Why can't you mind your own business? And that goes for the rest of you. None of you is worth a fart in a windstorm. So to hell with it." She got down from her stool and went off toward the back of the room.

Uncomfortable, Tully studied the cigarette-burned surface of the bar. A glass of port was set down by his hand. "Thanks."

"Don't mention it," said Earl. "I don't claim to be nothing more than I am. You maybe can fight, I'm an upholsterer."

"That's the way it goes."

"One man got muscles, another got steel. It all come out the same."

They drank in silence. When the woman returned, Tully rose and went out. He crossed the dark street to his hotel and limped up the stairs. On the bed in the dim light, hearing coughing from across the hall, he knew he had magnified Ernie Munger's talents. He had done it in order to go on believing in his body, but he had lost his reflexes—that was all there was to it—and he felt his life was coming to a close. At one time he had believed the nineteen-fifties would bring him to greatness. Now they were almost at an end and he was through. He turned onto his side. On the worn linoleum lay a *True Confession* and a *Modern Screen,* magazines he once would not have thought could interest him, but in reading of seduction and betrayal, adultery, divorce and the sorrows of stars, he found the sad sentiment of his love.

Tully had met his wife at Newby's Drive-Inn, a squat white building covered with black polka dots in the center of an expanse of asphalt shaded by mulberry trees. Despite the staining berries that had dropped on his yellow Buick convertible, he had gone there to see her every night. A carhop in tight black slacks and white blouse, she had presented a spectacular image. He could not stop thinking of her. Expensively dressed and winning fights, he felt he had to have her, and he was a proud husband, especially when she accompanied him to the local bouts, on the nights when he went as a spectator. Entering the auditorium on his arm, wearing knitted wool jersey—orange or white—or low-cut dresses held up by minuscule straps, in high backless shoes and with her long auburn hair piled on her head, she had roused the gallery to tumultuous shouting and whistling. He had come to expect it, walking in carrying her coat. That period had been the peak of his life, though he had not realized it then. It had gone by without time for reflection, ending while he was still thinking things were going to get better. He had not realized the ability and local fame he had then was all he was going to have. Nor had his manager realized it when he moved him up to opponents of national importance. That knowledge had been mercilessly pounded into Tully in a half dozen bouts as he swung and missed and staggered, eyes closed to slits. Then he had looked to his wife for some indefinable endorsement, some solicitous comprehension of the pain and sacrifice he felt he endured for her sake, some always withheld recognition of the rites of virility. Waiting, he drank. After six months he fought once more and was knocked out by a man of no importance at all. Then he began to wish for someone who could give him back that newly-wed wholeness and ease, but it was a feeling he could not find again, and he knew now that his mistake had been in thinking he could. That was how he had lost her—by looking for it. Without her he could not get up in the morning. He lost his job at the box factory and found another driving a truck. After he lost that too, the truck on its side in a ditch along with a hundred lugs of apricots, he lost his car. Now he brought an occasional woman to his room, but none of them could give him anything of his wife, and so he resented them all.

Since the receipt of the ominous papers referring to him as the defendant, as if his marital shortcomings had been criminal, Tully's only knowledge of his wife had come from her brother, Buck, whom he had met again one night on El Dorado Street between two shore patrolmen. A third-class petty officer, he appeared to have been strolling with the thirteen buttons of his fly open. Tully had hurried over and asked what had happened to Lynn. The patrolmen had ordered him to leave, an argument ensued, and Buck, between displays of defiance and submission, told him that Lynn was married to a Reno bartender. At the time the news had shaken Tully, yet he could not completely believe it. On these melancholy nights when he felt that only reconciliation could salvage his life, he believed she could not love anyone but him.

Shoes squeaked by outside the door. Reviewing old uncertainties and mistakes, Tully gazed down at the magazines. Finally he reached for the *Modern Screen* and propped himself up with his head between the rods of the bed. On the magazine's cover was an extravagantly smiling starlet in a bathing suit with a penciled dot over each breast and a scribbled cleft at the crotch. The coughing went on across the hall. It was time to change hotels.

2

The Lido Gym was in the basement of a three-story brick hotel with a façade of Moorish arches, columns, and brightly colored tile. Behind the hotel several cars, one tireless and up on blocks, rested among dry nettles and wild oats. In a long, narrow, open-end shed of weathered boards and corrugated steel, a group of elderly men were playing bocce ball with their hats on and arguing in Italian. A large paper bag in his hand, Ernie Munger went down the littered concrete stairs. In a ring under a ceiling of exposed joists, wiring, water and sewage pipes, a Negro was shadowboxing in the light of fluorescent tubes. Three men in street clothes, one bald, one with deeply furrowed cheeks, the third wearing a houndstooth-check hat with a narrow upturned brim, all turned their faces toward the door. The one with the deeply furrowed cheeks reached Ernie first.

"Want a fight, kid?"

"You Ruben Luna?"

"Gil Solis. How much you weigh? You got a hell of a reach. You looking for a trainer?"

They were joined by the man in the hat. A Mexican, as was Solis, he was perhaps forty, his face plump and relaxed, his skin smooth, his smile large, guileless and constant. "I'm Luna. You looking for me?"

"Yeah, I just thought I'd work out. Like to see what you think. Billy Tully told me I ought to come by."

"You know Tully?"

"I boxed with him the other day down at the Y."

"Is he getting in shape? How'd you do, all right? You must of done all right, huh?"

Now the bald man came over, whispering hoarsely, and Luna guided Ernie away with a hand on his shoulder. "Got your stuff there? We'll get you started." They walked on their heels through the shower room, the floor wet from a clogged drain. In a narrow, brick-walled, windowless room smelling of bodies, gym clothes and mildew, several partially dressed Negroes and Mexicans glanced up and went on conversing.

"Look around and find you an empty locker," said Luna. "Better bring a padlock with you next time. Get one of those combination kind. They're hard to pick. I'll be out in the gym when you get your togs on."

A service-station attendant, Ernie removed his leather jacket, oil-spotted khaki pants and shirt. When he came out into the gym in tennis shoes and bathing trunks, Ruben Luna sent him into the ring. With other shadowboxers maneuvering around him in intent mutual avoidance, their punches accented by loud snuffling, Ernie self-consciously warmed up.

"How'd you like to go a round or two?" Luna asked after he had called him out. "I'm not rushing you now. I'd just like to get a look at you."

"With who?"

"Beginner like you. Just box him like you did Tully. Colored boy over there."

Before a full-length mirror a boy in a Hawaiian-print bathing suit and white leather boxing shoes, his reddish hair straightened, was throwing punches.

Looking at those high white shoes, Ernie pushed his hands into heavy gloves held braced for him by the wrists. He stepped into a leather foulproof cup. A headguard was jerked over his brows. Padded and trussed, his face smeared with Vaseline, a rubber mouthpiece between his teeth, he stood waiting while two squat men punched and grappled in the ring. Then he was following his opponent's dark legs up the steps. For two rounds he punched, bounded and was hit in return, the headguard dropping over his eyes and the cup sagging between his legs. Afterward Ruben Luna leaned over the ropes, contending with Gil Solis for the headguard's buckle.

Stripped of the gloves, Ernie stood on the gym floor, panting and nodding while Ruben, squared off with his belly forward and hat brim up, moved his small hands and feet in quick and graceful demonstrations. "You got a good left. Understand what I mean? Step in with that jab. Understand what I mean? Get your body behind it. Bing! Understand what I mean? You hit him with that jab his head's going back, so you step in—understand what I mean?—hit him again, throw the right. Bing! Relax, keep moving, lay it in there, bing, bing, understand what I mean? Keep it out there working for you. Then feint the left, throw the right. Bing! Understand what I mean? Jab and feint, you keep him off balance. Feinting. You make your openings and step in. Bing, bing, whop! Understand what I mean?"

In the flooded shower room, Ernie was addressed by a small Mexican standing motionless under the other nozzle: "How's the ass up here?"

"Not good. Where you from?"

"L.A."

"How's the ass down there?"

"Good."

Soapless, the two hunched under the hissing spray.

"Are the guys tough in this town?"

"Not so tough. How about down there?"

"Tough."

"Just get here?"

"Yeah, I was in a bar yesterday, this guy's calling everybody a son-of-a-bitch. So I go out and wait for him. He come out and I ask did that include me. Says yeah. So I got him. I mean I just come to town. Some welcome. I don't know, trouble just seems to come looking for me."

Then the man began to sing, repeating a single phrase, his voice rising from bass moans and bellows to falsetto wails. *Earth Angel, Earth Angel, will you be mine?* The song went on in the locker room, the singer, as he put on his clothes, shifting to an interlude of improvisation: *Baby, baaaby, baaaaby, uh baby, uuh, oh yeauh, BAAAAAAABY, I WANT you,* while naked figures walked to and from the showers and steam drifted through the doorway. Drawing on his pants, Ernie, bruised, fatigued and elated, felt he had joined the company of men.

3

The bruises around Ernie's eyes faded from purple to greenish yellow and were superimposed by others. His lashes were rooted in blood-filled ridges, red welts marked the outer corners of each narrowed eye, there was a fatness to his nose. Yet Ruben Luna, observing from the ropes, knew this helmeted and heavy-gloved sparring in the gym was hardly fighting at all.

"Hit him. Don't apologize," he shouted, and Ernie nodded, once turning his head to listen and taking a punch. Assuming a classic pose, he circled and feinted, springing away from threatening gestures, then with no discernible reason, as if he had been waiting not for an opening but for inspiration, he charged, punching wildly. Every day, by another amateur or by the two professionals near his weight, one lighter, one heavier, both phlegmatic, his nose was bloodied.

Ruben watched patiently, believing in the eventual perfection of every promising move. He attended with towel and water bottle. Holding the heavy bag bucking against his chest, he coached with his cheek against the leather only a few inches from Ernie's smacking fists.

Concluding every workout he folded the towel into a pad, placed it on the floor, and while Ernie balanced on his head, bending his long neck from side to side, Ruben stood holding his ankles, gazing between the V of his legs off across the gym with the rapt eyes of a man whose reason for attention was ending for the day.

He went home to his family. Amid the arguing and nonsensical monologues of his children and the scolding of his wife, he ate his supper. He went to bed early and got up early, drove to the union hall, was dispatched with the gangs in the cold early light, and passed the day driving a forklift in the port. At noon he bought coffee and cupcakes from a girl in gabardine slacks who arrived every day in a snack truck. After work he drove across town to the gym, and in a coffee shop he was served pie by a tall blond waitress before crossing the street to his boxers.

"My white kid might shape up into something," he told his wife.

"That's good." Her hips wide in a sheer, peach-colored nightgown, her legs heavy and short, she was bending over, folding back the white satin bedspread. With a weary moan she crawled onto the bed and settled herself under the covers. Leaning against the upholstered headboard, she began creaming her face. There was a fullness to her brown throat, a softness under her chin. Her thick, wide, fierce lips that had once excited him sank at the corners into plump cheeks creased where there had once been dimples.

"He's got a great reach and a good pair of legs. And he's white, you know? He's a real clean good-looking kid. He could draw crowds some day if he could just fight. And maybe he can if he'd just listen. If I could put all I know in him he could make it. But I didn't learn it overnight either."

When his wife put away her jar and turned onto her side, pulling the covers up, Ruben began to undress. The room was lit by a bedside lamp, its shade enclosed in cellophane wrapping. On the dresser were a number of photos of his family, in frames and cardboard studio easels, among small boxes, ceramic figurines, and several bronze saddle horses of varying sizes standing on doilies. From one wall the serene face of Christ stared obliquely toward the back yard from a brass grillwork frame with a tiny burnt-out night light at the top.

In a pair of yellow pajamas, ripped under the arms and tight between the legs, Ruben got into bed. "I got nothing against coloreds," he said in the darkness. "Buford Wills is a good little colored boy, but there's too many in the game. Anglos don't want to pay to see two colored guys fight. They want a white guy. Like Tully. He was a pretty good draw. If he'd had a better punch he could of gone to the top. If he could of just hit harder and taken it a little better. He had everything else, but he let that bad streak discourage him. I guess he's getting in shape down there at the Y, though, or he wouldn't found this kid. He's got some miles left in him. This kid must of done good, too, and he could develop. He's tall for a welter. You ought to see the reach on him. If he put some weight on he could grow into a good-looking white heavyweight. Huh?" Ruben paused. "Victoria?" Unanswered, he felt his mood declining. What he had been saying now seemed foolish. In the isolation of his will, goaded by his back and shoulders, he felt the old urge to punch. Trying to sleep, he thought: I can't, I can't sleep. And he lunged over on his side, the feel of his wife's body, as it curved against his, as familiar as his own. "Sweetheart?" He patted her. "You awake?"

"Huh?"

"I was talking to you. Did you fall asleep?"

"What's the matter?"

"Nothing." He stroked her hip in atonement for waking her. "I just can't sleep."

"I don't think we should," she murmured.

Silent, he stilled his hand.

"Do you want to?" she whispered. "I think it's taking a chance."

"I know, I know."

"We could if you wanted to. I don't care."

"No, no, no. I don't care. I understand. That's not it. I'm just jumpy."

They lay quietly. Ruben's thoughts, diverted now, shifted to the snack-wagon driver. She was divorced, she had told him, and a mother of two children—a pleasant young woman whose friendliness he enjoyed as much as his glances at her snug gabardine slacks. But her children seemed a barrier and he began to think of the tall waitress across the street from the gym. She was reserved and had a look of sullenness. To her Ruben had spoken no more than his orders. He had looked at her behind the counter, leaning forward to see a little more, and that was all. But now she came to him with a forceful presence. He moved his hand over his wife, and the actual mass and possibility of her was strange and startling. Free of the mutual solicitude that kept him comfortable and subdued, he was aroused. His forehead wrinkling in concentration, he tried to keep the pale turgid nipples in his mind distinct from these flaccid bumps his children had suckled and that he, in the throes of excitement, had suckled too—a mimicry that had gone unmentioned, yet that even now, several years later, he felt had been wrong, a theft from his own babies and an abasement of a decent wife he did not deserve. Distracted, Ruben moved his hand down her belly, trying to realize that she was here offering herself up to him.

"You think it's all right?" she whispered, and the sense of peril unnerved and excited him. "You want to real bad?"

He no longer knew, wanting only quiet so the mass of her could regain that vivid reality. Silently addressing her with a name not her own, he persevered to a realm beyond all personality.

4

Days were like long twilights in the house under the black walnut trees; through untrimmed shrubs screening the windows the sun scarcely shone. It was a low, white frame house with a sagging porch roof supported by two chains that through years of stress had cracked the overhang of the main roof where they were attached, pulling it downward at so noticeable an angle that everything—overhang, chains, porch roof—appeared checked from collapsing by nothing more than the tar paper over the cracked boards. Inside, from other chains, hung light fixtures that never totally dispelled the murkiness of the rooms. At the back of the house, Ernie Munger slept late, stirring only briefly to the chatter of water pipes, subsiding back to sleep and waking at the banging of a frying pan, eating breakfast in his dreams before waking up at noon. Sluggish, he lay on his belly thinking of young divorcees and of a girl in a house in Isleton, a farm labor town he had visited one night with Gene Simms and a carload of acquaintances, its short main street in the shadow of the levee of the Sacramento River. It had been at the height of the harvest season; footsteps and fragments of Spanish passed constantly along the hall outside the room where he and his party waited with several stoical Filipinos smoking gnarled toscano cigars. They waited two hours before giving up. But before that ride home at a hundred and ten miles an hour between delta fields, the door to the room had opened once and Ernie had seen a girl of surprising loveliness. He had thought of her, a blonde in a pink formal, for several weeks before he returned one night alone. In another crowded room he waited for her, thinking he was at last going to know what it was, until the anticipation began to exhaust him. When he finally climbed with her to the top of the stairs, he confronted a woman at a table with a pan. The girl went on ahead while this matron in nurse's white made it clear what was expected of him. He balked, and at her first assisting touch his breath was stopped by the erratic pounding of his heart. Bathed by her antiseptic hands, he tried to resist the welling urgency, wanting to rush with his passion to the room where the girl was waiting, but he remained where he was, hopeless, the dismayed hygienist then calling down the hall: We had a little accident. He had not gone back again. Now he had developed a loyalty to Faye Murdock, a girl whose uncooperativeness excluded her from these morning reveries.

He ate breakfast alone—soft-boiled eggs, wholewheat toast, oranges and milk. By then his father, a tire recapper, would have finished half a day's work and his lunch. At the hour his father came home, Ernie was at the gym. From there he went to the service station and worked until two in the morning. He saw his father seldom, and though his mother was home all day, Ernie's association with her had long been only perfunctory. Short, impeded by her flesh, spreading and sagging from fifty years of gravity, hotcakes and pies, she showed on her face an almost constant expectation of mistake and mishap. Earlier in his life he had countered her worried curiosity with shouts of defiance. Now he eluded it with shifting eyes, shrugs and a completely unanimated face. After his first day at the Lido Gym he had taken a bottle of liquid make-up from the accumulation on her dressing table, and with it he hid his bruises from her as he and his sister, who had recently married with no advance warning, had long ago learned to conceal their private lives. As he grew older he had begun to feel that it was no longer his father but he whom she held responsible for a life that seemed to him perfectly natural for a mother. "Why don't you leave if you don't like it," he said to her one day in answer to a complaint encompassing the house, his father, his sister, himself, the entire town; and then her stricken face had filled him with anguish not only for what he had said but for the inconsiderate act of existing.

With a bowl and a carton of salt he retired to the bathroom. There he mixed a solution that he snuffed up his nostrils over the basin, a remedy Ruben Luna had recommended for toughening the interior of the nose. Sucked into his head, the warm salt water trickled down his throat. He choked, spat into the basin and, sneezing, sprayed his face in the mirror with blood-tinted drops. He snuffed in harsh handfuls, pinched his nostrils shut and dabbed the solution on his swollen brows, the make-up dissolving over his fingers like the pigment of his skin. He shook salt from the box and caked it on his eyelids and lips. When he released the brine from his outraged nose, cords of mucus dangled out after it. Sneezing and coughing, his eyes watering, he went on dabbing and snuffing.

Later he drove to the levee beside the river channel where freighters and tug-towed barges entered and left the port. Zipped up in his leather jacket, each fist squeezing a small rubber ball, he ran along the dirt road past burst mattresses, water heaters, fenders, sodden cartons, worn-out tires and rusty cans strewn down the steep bank. At the shore rocked bottles and driftwood, blackened tules, papers and occasionally a reeking, belly-up fish. Gulls turned in the gray sky and stood on piles across the channel. By the time Ernie was opposite the warehouses he was hot and sweaty. His breathing fixed to the plopping of his long black tennis shoes, he pounded past the port. As larks rose with flashes of yellow from the dead weeds and wild grass, sailed ahead, landed, sang their six tremulous notes, hushed and flew up once more, he came unflaggingly on, feeling he would never tire.

Where the channel forked off from the San Joaquin River the bank took a gradual turn. The oaks of Dad's Point stood ahead in the distance, their trunks painted white. Mouth gaping, his damp hair in his eyes, his body like a fired-up furnace, Ernie held his stride opposite Rough and Ready Island, where rows of moth-balled warships, their gun mountings sealed in protective pods, were moored three abreast for the

30

future. Gagging on a dry throat, he chose some object as his finish line and, plodding up to it on weighted legs, plodded right on past. His head back and his heaving chest shot with pains, he strained on to a farther landmark. He did not quit there either. He fought on with himself to the edge of the park and, stumbling over the lawn past picnic tables and barbecue pits, careened with flailing arms farther and farther under the trees, until at last he stood gasping on the muddy bank of the point with nowhere else to run.

5

The gym was open when Ruben Luna arrived with Ernie Munger, who went on to the locker room. Gil Solis and Babe Azzolino stood idly by the ring with their hands in their pockets, their faces expressive only of suspended emotion as they waited for their athletes.

"I just took the kid down and bought him his license," Ruben said, joining them.

"That right?" Babe's straining voice, impaired by Adam's-apple punches, was little more than a hoarse, penetrating whisper. Short, trim, his snub face thrust forward now with a look of intense concentration, the remnants of his black, oiled hair combed back from the temples, he rocked on his toes, jingling change in his yellow-ochre slacks.

"What if he quits?" asked Gil. "You're out your five bucks."

"He won't quit. You know what the doctor said about him?"

"Look what Castillo did to me." Gil's tense, lined face was bitter. "You know how much money I gave that guy? I bet I use to give him a dollar every day. Two dollars, three dollars. Nearly every damn day. And he run off on me. Every day it was movies. Movies. I was always digging in my pocket for that guy and he takes off back to Mexico. Know what he is now? Know what he is? Number ten."

"You should of done something right at the time," Babe gasped, his voice croaking, breaking.

"What could I do?"

"You should of gone right to a lawyer."

"Yeah," said Ruben. "I took the kid to the doctor and he thought the needle was dull. He wanted to get some blood, you know, but it don't go in."

Gil hoisted his pants. "I know one thing, I'm not loaning any more money. Needle was dull, huh?"

"No, no, it was a good needle. So you know what he says?"

"Well, he probably had a dull needle."

"No, he tried two needles."

"Who's this?" whispered Babe. "The kid?"

"Yeah, I took him down and got him his license to-day, and the doctor could hardly get a needle in him."

"What was the matter, dull needle?"

"The kid's like leather."

"That's odd, Ruben. That's odd. Let me tell you that's odd. I wouldn't of thought that looking at him. Yeah, that's odd. Manny Chavez had thick skin, you know, but he was tough, you guys know that, I mean they don't come like him every day."

"That's not half of it. Hold on. He finally gets the needle in, see, and gets the blood and it's almost black."

"I had Chavez down in L.A. against Montoya—first round he gets butted over the eye and the blood starts running and I think well there goes the fight. But it's not his blood, it's Montoya's. He's got a cut on the top of his head must of took ten stitches. Chavez didn't have a mark on him."

"Remember that guy Estrada?" interrupted Gil. "I seen him open a Coke bottle with his teeth."

"The hell you say. They break?"

"Listen, I didn't tell you the half of it. The doctor gets the blood out, it's black, and he's just staring at it when I ask him to burn the veins out of the kid's nose —stop those nosebleeds. So he puts the blood down a minute and gets his spark gun and when he gets done burning his nose out he picks up the tube again and turns it upside down to have another look and the blood in it don't even run down. It just kind of stays up at the top of the tube. It's turned to gelatin."

Gil dug thoughtfully between his buttocks. Ruben sighed, made a few aimless sputters with his lips and began to hum. Babe cleared his ruined throat. "Manny Chavez," he whispered, "had the clearest piss of any man I ever seen. He'd take a specimen and the piss in that bottle would be just as clean and pure as fresh drinking water."

6

On the day before Ernie's first bout, he drove with Faye Murdock out of town and across the Calaveras River—brown and high from the rains—and turned down a lane that ran parallel to the levee. At a dirt turnoff used by lovers and fishermen, he drove up onto the levee and parked out of sight of housing tracts while dull-gray mud hens flapped away in the late afternoon, running over the water as they flew. Dark clouds extended to the horizon. Along the muddy banks of the river, red-wing blackbirds sang in the cattails. His arms around Faye, as before on so many other untraveled roads, Ernie whispered and blew in her small bitter ear.

Faye was a solemn dark-haired girl with large attractive teeth, fair skin, and a short fleshy body that seemed to Ernie impervious to stimulation. He had begun taking her out because for a time she had gone with Steve Bonomo, whose success with a previous girl Ernie had read about on the wall of a high school lavatory. His first time alone with Faye, Ernie had sensed a difference from the other crossed-legged girls he had dated.

He felt in her lips and arms a lonely employment of him. Doggedly his campaign had gone on until he and Faye were among those who cruised under the lights of Main Street in predictable, faithful pairs, the dense one-way traffic proceeding slowly through yellow lights, blocking the street to cross traffic, the riders conversing from car to car while horns blared, the procession starting off again with squealing tires and rapping pipes only to brake, lurching, once again to a creeping mass. Yet, for all his fidelity, Ernie remained as frustrated as the young men who cruised alone or in groups as he had once cruised, looking for that mythical female pedestrian who would like to go for a ride.

The sky darkened, the liquid singing of the blackbirds diminished and ceased, mud hens swam back to shore, climbed up the banks and huddled in the willows. The lights of a farm came on in the brown distance where patches of tule fog lay on the barren muddy fields. A wind came with the darkness, rattling the license plate, and a low, honking flight of geese passed.

Later in the night it began to rain. To Ernie the first patters were like small sounds from Faye's mouth. Her lips had been against his so long that his mind was drifting among images of reeds wavering with the delicate movements of her tongue. When the roof began drumming, they sat up. Rain was pouring over the windshield, battering the ground, hissing into the invisible river. Ernie opened the window and the cold rain blew against his face. From his hunger he realized that many hours had gone by. In the light of a match, Faye's wan and tired face, the downward angle of the cigarette, her rumpled clothes, unpinned hair, and the slump of her neck renewed his hopes.

Within closed steamy windows an embrace went on like the same endless moment, broken only by an occasional digestive murmur and Faye's lighting of cigarettes. Finally, in his weariness, Ernie began to accept that once again he had been baffled. There was no consolation from having tried everything he could think of. To appear in a ring tomorrow without ever having won this other battle seemed presumptuous and dangerous. He alone in the Lido Gym carried a burden of silence and deceptive innuendo, and he wondered if this could mean the difference between victory and defeat. He was persevering with his repertory of foreplay, which nothing else ever followed, when Faye's fingers came to rest on his thigh, over the small tin box in his pocket.

"Aspirin?"

Alarmed, he gave no answer, and uncertain what he should do, he allowed her hand into the pocket. She withdrew the box and he heard it click open in the darkness. As the silence continued he sagged against the door. The box snapped shut and was replaced.

"Were you planning it all this time?"

"No."

"You always carry them?"

"It was just in case something came up."

"You mean if you couldn't use them on me you'd use them on whoever would let you?"

"I wouldn't want anybody but you."

"What made you think I'd do it?"

"I was just hoping."

"Is that all you think I am?"

"What do you mean? We haven't even done it."

"You want to, though. Is that all you think about?"

"I don't think about that at all."

"You just said that's what you were hoping."

He thought a moment. "I just want what we'd both enjoy."

"Oh, sure."

For a while neither spoke, and Ernie wondered if he had talked his way clear.

"Do you really care for me?" she asked at last.

There was a silence so heady that he began to tremble. "I guess I'm in love," he answered, and slumped lower in fear of what he had said. Had he committed himself for nothing, or had he only said the one thing he should have said all along? The rain beat on the roof. They were sitting apart; he did not know now if she would even let him touch her, but unable to think of anything else, afraid the opportune moment might be passing, he reached out to her and she moved into his arms. It was as if the air had been knocked out of him. She clung to him and he contorted, suffocating, kicking the door as he tried to maneuver, knowing beyond all doubt that the inevitable moment had at last arrived. He pulled at her clothing, pushed her down on the seat. He sprawled, he thrust a foot through the spokes of the steering wheel. There was a smack of flesh. As Ernie's eyes pinched shut he felt the pulse of ecstatic oblivion and the horn began to honk.

In a moment all was still. Collapsed, conscious again

of the rain on the roof, he realized he had experienced the ultimate in pleasure.

"Was it good?" he asked.

"It was nice," whispered Faye.

Ernie was gratified, hearing that. Still he was uncertain. He wondered if everything had gone as it should. Was that all there was to it? Perhaps it had been celebrated out of proportion because there was nothing else to live for. He lay with his face in a split in the seat, his nose squashed against the stuffing.

"It must be getting late."

"Yeah."

"Are we all right here?"

"We better go," he murmured into the seat.

"Do you think we should?"

He abruptly sat up. "We better get out of here."

"Maybe we shouldn't have stayed so long."

The engine rumbled, the lights shone out into the rain, the wipers swept and clacked across the windshield. After a few yards the car stopped, wheels spinning in the mud. Ernie shifted from low to reverse, trying to rock free, but the tires dug in and settled firmly.

"What'll we do? I should have gone home," said Faye.

Glad to get away from her, he stepped out into the rain. Leaving her at the wheel, he grasped the rear bumper, his back to the car, his shoes gripped by mud. Shouting directions, he heaved forward. The car thrust backward. He leaped away, screaming above the whining wheels. She shifted and the engine died.

"I can't do it," she said and he was afraid she was

going to cry. Face streaming, he got back in to start the engine. "I wish we hadn't come," she said. "I wish I'd stayed home."

Ernie returned to the rear bumper. While the tires sprayed mud, he grunted and pushed and yelled at her not to spin the wheels. Finally, feet sucking and splashing, he walked off in search of boards, crashing angrily through the bushes down the steep slope of the levee. He was close to the water now but could not see it. In front of him was a black expanse with a sound like escaping steam. As he felt around on the bank he heard Faye calling from the car and he bellowed back, disgusted that she thought he would run off in the rain and leave her. Whipped by twigs, he was pulling himself along the bank from willow to willow when a whirring of wings rushed up before him. Recoiling, he slipped, throwing out his hands, striking the ground on his side, and instantly he was in the icy shock of the river, up to his waist, disbelieving, tearing away chunks of bank in terror. Blindly he clambered out and stood quaking on the slick bank, his teeth chattering, water pouring from his pants and his shoes full. Clutching twigs, his mind assailed by that black immersion, by what had happened in the car, he felt that everything had passed out of his control. He had to get home, had to get warm and dry and rested for his fight, but he was out here, wet in the bushes, stuck miles from town with a girl he might now never be able to get rid of. Through the hissing rain his horn sounded. Ernie moved ahead along the bank, weighed down by his pants.

He returned to the car dragging a waterlogged board.

"Ernie? Is that you?"

"Who else? What's all the noise about?"

"I was afraid you got lost."

Cursing, he jammed the board under the rear tire. He pushed, the wheels spun, the board cracked, the car surged ahead and mired down, Ernie collapsing in the glow of the taillights. Wallowing on his knees, he dug at the mud, jammed the cracked board back under the tire, and heaved against the car while Faye raced the engine. When they at last reached firm ground near the point where the levee road turned down again to the paved lane, the car lurched and careened ahead. Ernie ran after it down the turnoff.

"Will you call me tomorrow?" Faye asked on the way back to town.

"What for?"

"Because I want to talk to you."

Feeling the obligations already beginning, he agreed.

Her street was submerged from curb to curb, the water roaring under the car as they approached her house. Her porch light was the only one on in the block.

7

A carload of boxers departed in the rain. They rode past the county hospital, past leafless vineyards, orchards and walnut groves, barns, chicken pens and puddle-covered fields. On the back seat, slumped between Wes Haynes and Buford Wills—both wearing small black hats with upturned brims—sat Ernie Munger. Ruben Luna was driving. Beside him Babe Azzolino rode with Bobby Burgos, a Filipino bantamweight, who was his only fighter of the night. While the two managers talked on and on, Ernie nodded, dozed and jerked awake.

"We got the winners," said Ruben. "What do you think?"

"I'd say we got the winners."

"We got four sure winners. You know what I'd like to do some day? I'd like to take these guys to England. They appreciate class over there. When I turn these boys pro I'd really like to make that trip."

In Salinas they had a dinner of chili burgers. "This guy can't fight," said Ruben, sitting across from Ernie in the booth. "You'll knock him out. How you feel? Hardly wait to get in there?"

"I'll give it all I got," said Ernie.

"You may have to go the four rounds, so don't punch yourself out. Don't lose your head."

"I won't. I'll pace myself."

"It goes fast, though, so don't hang back."

"I won't hang back. I'll give it everything I got."

"Yeah, but you want to pace yourself. Buford, your guy's been around so you don't want to let him get a good shot at you. But he's a boozer, you know how these soldiers are. He won't go the limit."

Fog was blowing above the roofs and trees when they reached Monterey. Del Monte Gardens was near the edge of town. Ruben Luna, leaning slightly backward, coat and sweater unbuttoned, shirt open at the throat, hat back and arms swinging, led the way in. Several boxers were already in the dressing room, resting on tables, undressing, moving nervously around amid a murmur of voices and tense clearing of noses. Lightheaded from hours on the road, Ernie listlessly took off his clothes. In new boxing shoes, leather cup and a pair of purple-trimmed gold trunks with a monogrammed A, he shifted about while Ruben wrapped his hands, moving with him, winding the gauze and muttering to him to keep still. With narrow strips of adhesive, the bandages were taped down and anchored between each finger. The gloves Ruben pulled first onto his own hands, pounding and kneading the padding away from the knuckles before he removed them and, braced, held them for Ernie to work on. They were smaller than those Ernie had trained with, and he shuffled in his light shoes, swinging his arms while Ruben pursued him, smearing Vaseline around his eyes

43

and down the bridge of his nose. Ruben then crossed the room to Wes Haynes, who was sitting in T-shirt and jockstrap on the edge of a table, his red straightened hair in a high mound.

"I just hope I didn't leave my fight in the bedroom," Ernie confided to Buford Wills. Buford, matched for the semi-final, was still in his street clothes. "Don't tell Ruben this, but I was out getting a little last night."

"I was too. That don't make no difference. It don't matter if you dead drunk, you got two hands you can beat that motherfucker. I don't care who he is. It all in your mind."

"I hope so."

"Hoping never done nothing. It *wanting* that do it. You got to want to win so bad you can taste it. If you want to win bad enough you win. They no way in hell this dude going beat me. He too old. I going be all over him. I going kick his ass so bad, every time he take a bite of food tomorrow he going think of me. He be one sore son-of-a-bitch. He going *know* he been in a fight. I get him before he get me. I going hit him with everything. I won't just *beat* that motherfucker, I going *kill* him." Buford was small and thin. His hair, divided at one side with a razor-blade part, was cropped close. His nose turned up, his nostrils flared, his lips were soft and full and his hooded eyes were narrowed in a constant frown. The year before, only fourteen, he had lied about his age and won the Golden Gloves novice flyweight title in San Francisco. Tonight he was fighting the champion of Fort Ord. "You want to know what make a good fighter?"

"What's that?"

"It believing in yourself. That the will to win. The rest condition. You want to kick ass, you kick ass."

"I hope you're right."

"You don't want to kick ass, you get your own ass whipped."

"I want to kick ass. Don't worry about that."

"You just shit out of luck."

"I said I wanted to kick ass."

"You got to want to kick ass *bad*. They no manager or trainer or pill can do it for you."

"I want to kick ass as bad as you do."

"Then you go out and kick ass."

"All right." Ernie moved away, irritated with his deferring to a boy. Lethargically he bobbed and shuffled. When his name was called through the doorway, he began wildly shadowboxing.

"Hold off. You'll wear yourself out. We got to go on now," said Ruben. "Babe, get the towels, get the towels."

"I didn't get a chance to warm up," Ernie complained.

"That's okay, you're ready. Just stay loose. Where's the bucket?"

"I got the bucket in my hand," whispered Babe. He was dressed in russet slacks, a yellow knit shirt and a moss-green cardigan sweater with a towel over one shoulder.

"Got the bottle?"

"The bottle's right here in the bucket."

"You put the water in it?"

"I wouldn't bring an empty bottle."

"I'm just asking. I don't want to bring my kid out there without any water."

"I got the damn water. Take it easy. I told you I got the water."

The three went out into the crowd. The referee, a short, bald, heavy man in gray, was leaning back with outspread arms on the ropes. A towel around his shoulders, Ernie scuffed his shoes in the resin box under the blazing lights. When he went to his corner, Ruben gripped the back of his neck and tried to shove the teeth protector into his mouth. Resisting, Ernie broke away and spit out his gum.

The bell tolled in summons. Whistles, restive clapping, echoed in the arena. At last a Mexican in a brilliant red robe jogged down the aisle, followed by his handlers. Ducking through the ropes, he caught a foot, and his lunge into the ring was converted to prancing and shadowboxing, a second scurrying after him attempting to untie the robe.

"Good," said Ruben. "You got the reach."

His name was Manuel Rosales. At the scattered applause given its announcement, Ernie was uneasy; but at his own introduction there was the same tribute to his merely being here in trunks. Ruben and Babe were out of the ring now but their massaging hands were still on him. The house lights went off and Rosales faced him across the white canvas. Startled by the bell and a shove against his back, Ernie bounded forward. His opponent turned around in his corner, went down on one knee and crossed himself. He rose immediately, his hair, in a grown-out crew cut, standing up like a wild boar's bristles. The two touched gloves across the referee's arm. Ernie, embarrassed about hitting Rosales so soon after prayer, reached out to touch gloves again and was struck on the side of the head. Offended, he lashed out and felt the thrilling impact of bone through the light gloves. Stirred by shouts, amazed by his power over the crowd, he sprang in, punching, and was jolted by a flurry. He backed off. Chewing on the mouthpiece, he danced around the ring while Rosales charged after him, swinging and missing. The referee maneuvered his nimble bulk out of their way, and the opposing seconds shouted unheeded instructions.

"Jab! Throw the right! Throw the right! Jab! One-two!"

"Pégale! Tírale al cuerpo! Abajo! Abajo!"

Between rounds Ruben coached with a ruthless expression Ernie had never seen on him before, his arms sometimes punching out in demonstrations.

"Step in and nail him. Understand what I mean?"

"Hook," croaked Babe, leaning through the ropes with the tape-covered water bottle.

At the bell, Ruben's hands were at Ernie's buttocks, heaving him up off the stool, and when Ernie came back after a round of dancing and jabbing, he was hit in the face with a wet sponge. He was rubbed, patted, squeezed and kneaded. Cold water was poured into his trunks. He was harangued, he was reprimanded, and he listened to nothing at all. As he stood up, the towel passed under his nose and he recoiled from the fumes of ammonia.

His lead sent a shower flying from Rosales' hair. He stepped away and Rosales hurled himself into the ropes.

"Go in! He's tired, he's tired, he's tired!" Ruben yelled, and Ernie realized he was tired too. He struck out and moved away. Backed into a corner, he was attempting to clinch when a blinding blow crushed his nose. Bent over with his arms around Rosales' waist, he became aware of the referee tugging on him. Locked together, the three staggered about, blood spattering their legs, until Ernie's grasp was broken.

Blearily he saw a gush of blood down his chest. The referee was holding him, looking up at his eyes. "I'm okay, I'm okay," Ernie said through a throbbing nose and began to understand that something was wrong with him. Afraid the fight was going to be stopped, he pushed toward Rosales, there openmouthed behind the referee, his gleaming body splashed with blood. He was blocked. He lunged, but the referee, his face fat and red above the black bow tie, was pressing him back, his fingers fumbling for the mouthpiece. Ernie turned his head from side to side, dodging his hand and protesting through the rubber: "Shit, I'm okay. Shit, goddamn it, I'm okay." Then Ruben was in the ring, holding him by the shoulders.

"Tilt your head back. Breathe through your mouth."

He was being sponged in his corner when his opponent, now back in the red robe, came over, mumbling, to hang an arm briefly around his neck.

"Look to me like he butted you," whispered Babe after Rosales had gone back across the spotted canvas.

"I don't know what it was."

"Sure he butted you. Because he can't punch," said Ruben, and he went to the referee.

With his hand on the back of Ernie's neck, Ruben

complained loudly up the aisle to the dressing room, where Buford Wills sat lost in the folds of a royal-blue robe and Wes Haynes stood waiting in gloves, white shoes and jockstrap.

"You lose, huh?"

"He wasn't hurt at all. It should never been stopped."

Ernie's gloves were pulled off and the handwraps cut away with hasty precision. A gray-haired manager came and peered at his nose.

"You want to get a note from the doctor before you leave. You can get that nose set tomorrow and it won't cost you nothing."

"He was butted. They should throw that kid out of the ring."

Ernie removed the trunks and cup and they were given to Wes Haynes. Grumbling, he put them on. "They all bloody," he objected to Ruben.

"That's all right. It's not your blood."

Ernie was left standing with his head tilted back. Blood still trickling over his lips, he went to a mirror. His nose looked like a boiled sausage about to burst. He went into the shower room and, feeling the pulse of splintered bone, stood with closed eyes under the spray.

49

8

Wes Haynes had not lasted a round. Hurling himself forward with a right swing, he had run into a cross to the jaw. Then wildly pummeled, he had crouched against the ropes with his gloves cupped before his face, unsure of what to do and so merely waiting for his opponent to stop hitting him so that he could start hitting again himself. But when the punches ceased he looked up to find the fight had been stopped. Mortified before so many witnesses, he had shaken his head as though truly dazed.

In the dressing room afterwards, Wes had remained close to Buford Wills. He sat next to him in the car. In a Mexican café in Salinas he was next to him still, their dark fists side by side on the table, each holding a bottle of orange soda. Buford had been outboxing the flyweight champion of Fort Ord until knocked senseless in the final round, and now Ruben glanced at him, inquiring with a cheerfulness Wes could see was forced: "Doing all right? How you feel?"

"Just pissed off," said Buford.

"You dropped your left. Don't sweat over it. You'll

get him again. They'll have you back and you'll knock him out next time. He don't have what he use to have. Ernie, you'll get that nose set as good as new, don't worry about it. Look at mine. Would you believe mine was ever busted?"

"Yeah."

"I don't know what kind of deal we were getting there tonight, but I never seen anything like it. Stopping that fight when Ernie had the guy beat. You saw it, Babe. That kid should of been disqualified. Wes wasn't hurt either. Anybody can get tagged the first round. You take a good punch like Wes does, it don't mean a thing. And Bobby, he won every round."

"He did," Babe agreed. "That's a fact. That was robbery if I ever seen it. You were hurting that boy."

"What difference it make?" Scowling, his broad, tan face unmarked, Bobby Burgos took a drink from his bottle of beer.

If you guys was any kind of trainers, look like one of us ought to won, thought Wes.

Babe called in vain for the waitress, his voice failing under the exertion, his cries like the desperate nasal mumbling of a mute. Ruben turned, said "Hey," and she approached.

"Sweetheart, give us some more beer, and some pop for these boys."

"I want a beer, too," said Wes, sulking. "I don't want no *pop*. Want a Lucky Lager. I'm twenty-two."

"I can't help it. If you had an ID I'd serve you."

"Left it home." Wrinkling his forehead, Wes, seventeen, looked her in the face as if to invite closer scrutiny.

"This one's all right," she said to Ruben, nodding toward Bobby Burgos. "It's just these three."

"We been through all this," said Ruben. "Forget it. Pop's better for them anyway. Wes, sure you don't want another one? Bring him another pop. These boys fought their hearts out tonight over at the Del Monte Gardens."

"What are they, boxers?"

"These boys are the top amateurs in the Valley. We come all the way up from Stockton. You like fights? Come with us sometime. I'll get you in free."

"She's married," said Babe, drawing on a thin cigar.

"How do you know?"

"Ring."

"That's all right. Your husband wouldn't mind if you went to the fights one night, would he?"

She laughed evasively, and as she walked away with the empty bottles, Ruben said: "Nice ass."

"How old you think *she* is?" asked Wes.

"She's old enough. She's old enough."

"Shit. I wish I could get her out in the car," said Wes. "I'd fuck her to death."

Wes Haynes had drunk four bottles of soda by the time they went out. They drove along the highway until a neon cocktail glass appeared in the darkness. By then Buford was asleep. Wes remained with him in the car. When the others finally came out of the bar, Ruben got in back, and the motor droned on into the night. Jolted awake, the car momentarily off onto the shoulder then swerving back onto the pavement, Wes saw flat misty fields, fences, barns, the dark contours of distant hills. Waking again to the faint sound of music, the motor silent, only Babe and Bobby gone from the car, the others sleeping, Wes saw a low building in the fog with *Regal Pale* glowing in blue neon in a window and was overcome with dejection. He had made no secret of his training. Acquaintances at school spoke to him as though they believed he was a professional, and he had not cared to correct them. He had believed he would be one soon enough—because it had seemed the natural and inevitable thing for so many years, because against all contrary evidence, and simply because he was himself, he felt he could never be dominated. Now he felt he should have known all along that he was nothing. Boxers were men in other towns, in big cities far from this car parked in the darkness alongside the highway between fields of vegetables. Resting his cheek against the cold window, he thought of killing himself, but years ago, standing beside his father's legs in a crowd on a night sidewalk, he had seen a dead man profiled in a puddle of blood, his eye dumfounded, and Wes knew that if he was going to be killed he was not going to do it himself. They would have to come and get him and he would club them and choke them and shoot them and then he would run.

The voice of Bobby Burgos approached as if arguing with itself. Not until the voice reached the car did Wes hear Babe's hoarse replies. "I'll whip your ass. I'm not going to let you behind that wheel. I'll take you on right now. Put up your hands. Don't you believe me? I'm not going to let you behind that wheel. It's Ruben's car, I can't be responsible for letting you behind that wheel. I'm sorry, old buddy, but that's the way it is."

The interior light came on and as Babe crawled in, Burgos gave him a shove that sent him across the seat and against Ernie Munger, who sat suddenly upright.

"Don't get smart," warned Babe.

"Just shut up." The door slammed. In a moment the engine started.

"Don't drive too fast, Burgos. I'll nail you one."

"Man, I'm not going to drive fast. You're the one was driving too fast."

"I wasn't driving fast."

"Hundred's pretty fast."

"I wasn't going a hundred."

"You were all over the road. You're drunk as a pig."

"What? What am I? What did you say to me?" asked Babe. And they were off again down the highway, Buford's small lax body vibrating against Wes in the drone of the motor that for moments faded to silence as if the car were still back in the parking area outside the bar with the blue neon sign.

Wes awoke on a street of small frame houses. The driver's seat was empty. All was silent except for the snores and snuffles of damaged noses. Shivering from the cold, his mind stark and confused, Wes got out to look up and down the wet street for Bobby Burgos. There was nowhere he could have gone, no bar or café or gas station, not even a lighted porch. Wes found himself at the corner looking down another street just as deserted. He looked back at the car; there was no one in sight anywhere. Burgos had vanished. A heavy mist was falling, making a nimbus around each streetlight. His face wet, his straightened hair standing upright from moisture and sleep, Wes looked up at the low, drizzling sky. Where he was he had no idea, but it was a town he had never seen before. He returned to the car and waited behind the steering wheel for Burgos.

"Bobby gone," he said aloud. "Where's Bobby?" But no one in the car answered and the sound of his voice made him uneasy. Finally he started the motor, thinking the sound might summon Burgos from wherever he was, but the idling motor seemed to make the car the focus of all the stillness of the street. He did not honk the horn. He put the car into gear and drove off. Afraid he might be unable to find the place again where Burgos had vanished, Wes looked at the names on the street signs. Before long he began to notice a familiar sequence. Driving slowly on, he waited to see if the name of his own street would come up in its proper order as had the names of the others; and seeing it, he turned mechanically, continuing along with that same suspension of thought until he was parked before his own house, the simulated tan bricks of its asphalt siding already faintly discernible.

"Buford, we home." Leaning over the seat, he shook the thin leg.

"Uh."

"We in Stockton. You want to drive the rest of the way? I'm going to bed."

"Don't know how."

"Ruben? Ruben, hey, wake up, we home. Ruben?"

"Okay."

"You awake?"

"Oh, yeah, everything's fine."

"I leave it to you then." Wearing his hat and carrying

his bag, Wes went around the house to the back door. He felt his way to his room, undressed to the sound of his brothers' even breathing, got into bed and lay waiting. He heard nothing. Soon he rose and tiptoed to the front room, where he looked out the window and saw the car still there, clear in the first light of dawn that filled him with all the desolate reality of defeat. Quietly, in dread of waking his family, Wes crept back to his bed.

9

Hundreds of men were on the lamplit street, lined for blocks with labor buses, when Billy Tully arrived, still drunk. He had been up most of the night, as he had nearly every other night since the loss of his cook's job; and he had been fired because of absences following nights out drinking. It had been agony getting up after three hours' sleep. After the night clerk's pounding, Tully had remained motionless, shaken, hearing the knocking at other doors, the same hoarse embittered summons down the hall. It had been so demoralizing that he had taken his bottle out with him under the morning stars. In the other pocket of his gray zipper jacket were two sandwiches in butcher paper. He had eaten no breakfast.

The wine calmed his shivering as he passed the dilapidated buses, the hats and sombreros and caps of the men inside silhouetted in the windows. The drivers stood by the doors addressing the crowds.

"Lettuce thinners! Two more men and we're leaving."

"Onion toppers, over here, let's go."

"Cherries! First picking."

"They ripe?"

"Sure they're ripe."

"How much you paying?"

"A man can make fifteen, twenty dollars a day if he wants to work."

"Shit, who you kidding?"

"Pea pickers!"

The sky was still black. Only a few lights were on in the windows of the hotels, dim bulbs illuminating tattered shades and curtains, red fire-escape globes. Under the streetlights the figures in ragged overalls, army fatigues, khakis and suit coats all had a somber uniformity. They pushed to board certain buses that quickly filled and rolled away, grinding and backfiring, and in these crowds Billy Tully jostled and elbowed, asking where the buses were going and sometimes getting no answer. He crossed the street, which was crossed continuously by the men and the few women and by trotting preoccupied dogs, and stopped at a half-filled sky-blue bus with dented fenders and a fat young man in jeans at the door.

"Onions. Ever topped before?"

"Sure."

"When was that?"

"Last year."

"Get on."

Tully climbed into the dark shell, his shoes contacting bottles and papers, and waited amid the slumped forms while the driver recruited outside. "If these onions were any good," Tully said, "looks like he could get him a busload."

"They better than that damn short-handle hoe."

"Maybe I ought to go pick cherries."

"You make more topping onions, if we can get this man moving."

The stars paled, the sky turned a deep clear blue. Trucks and buses lurched away. The crowd outside thinned and separated into groups.

"Let's get going, fat boy," Tully yelled.

"Driver, come *on*. I got in this bus to top onions and I want to top onions. I'm an onion-topping fool."

The bus rattled past dark houses, gas stations, neon-lit motels, and the high vague smokestack of the American Can Company, past the drive-in movie, its great screen white and iridescent in the approaching dawn, across an unseen creek beneath ponderous oaks, past the cars and trailers and pickup-truck caravans of the gypsy camp on its bank and out between the wide fields. Near a red-and-white-checkered *Purina Chows* billboard, it turned off the highway. Down a dirt road it bumped to a barn, and the crew had left the bus and taken bottomless buckets from a pickup truck when the grower appeared and told them they were in the wrong man's onion field. The buckets clattered back into the truckbed, the crew returned to the bus, and the driver, one sideburn hacked unevenly and a bloodstained scrap of toilet paper pasted to his cheek, drove back to the highway swearing defensively while the crew cursed him among themselves. The sky bleached to an almost colorless lavender, except for an orange glow above the distant mountains. As the blazing curve of the sun appeared, lighting the faces of the men jolting in the bus—Negro paired with Negro, white with white, Mexican with Mexican and Filipino beside Filipino—

Billy Tully took the last sweet swallow of Thunderbird, and his bottle in its slim bag rolled banging under the seats.

They arrived at a field where the day's harvesting had already begun, and embracing an armload of sacks, Tully ran with the others for the nearest rows, stumbling over the plowed ground, knocking his bucket with a knee in the bright onion-scented morning. At the row next to the one he claimed knelt a tall Negro, his face covered with thin scars, his knife flashing among the profusion of plowed-up onions. With fierce gasps, Tully removed his jacket and jerked a sack around his bottomless bucket. He squatted, picked up an onion, severed the top and tossed the onion as he was picking up another. When the bucket was full he lifted it, the onions rolling through into the sack, leaving the bucket once again empty.

In the distance stood the driver, hands inside the mammoth waist of his jeans, yelling: "Trim those bottoms!"

There was a continuous thumping in the buckets. The stooped forms inched in an uneven line, like a wave, across the field, their progress measured by the squat, upright sacks they left behind. In the air was a faint drone of tractors, hardly audible above the hum that had been in Tully's ears since his first army bouts a decade past.

He scrabbled on under the arc of the sun, cutting and tossing, onion tops flying, the knife fastened to his hand by draining blisters. Knees sore, he squatted, stood, crouched, sat, and knelt again and, belching a stinging taste of bile, dragged himself through the morning. By noon he had sweated himself sober. Covered with grime, he waddled into the bus with his sandwiches and an onion.

"You got you a nice onion for lunch," a Negro woman remarked through a mouthful of bread, and roused to competition, an old, grizzled, white man, with the red inner lining exposed on his sagging lower lids, brought from under his jacket on the seat his own large onion.

"Ain't that a beauty?" All the masticating faces were included in his stained and rotting smile. "Know what I'm going to do with it? I'm going to take that baby home and put it in vinegar." He covered it again with his jacket.

Out in the sun the scarred Negro at the row beside Tully's worked on in a field now almost entirely deserted.

Through the afternoon heat the toppers crawled on, the rows of filled sacks extending farther and farther behind. The old grizzled man, half lying near Tully, his face an incredible red, was still filling buckets though he appeared near death. But Tully was standing. Revived by his lunch and several cupfuls of warm water from the milk can, he was scooping up onions from the straddled row, wrenching off tops, ignoring the bottom fibrils where sometimes clods hung as big as the onions themselves, until a sack was full. Then he thoroughly trimmed several onions and placed them on top. Occasionally there was a gust of wind and he was engulfed by sudden rustlings and flickering shadows as a high spiral of onion skins fluttered about him like a swarm of butterflies. Skins left

61

behind among the discarded tops swirled up with delicate clatters and the high, wheeling column moved away across the field, eventually slowing, widening, dissipating, the skins hovering weightlessly before settling back to the plowed earth. Overhead great flocks of rising and falling blackbirds streamed past in a melodious din.

In the middle of the afternoon the checkers shouted that the day's work was over.

Back in the bus, glib and animated among the workers he had surpassed, the Negro who had topped next to Tully shouted: "It easy to get sixty sacks."

"So's going to heaven."

"If they onions out there I get me my sixty sacks. I'm an onion-topping fool. Now I mean onions. I don't mean none of them little pea-dingers. Driver, let's go get paid. I don't want to look at, hear about, or smell no more onions till tomorrow morning, and if I ain't there then hold the bus because I'm a sixty-sack man and I just won't quit."

"Wherever you go there's always a nigger hollering his head off," muttered the old man beside Tully.

"Just give me a row of good-size onions and call me happy."

"You can have them," said Tully.

"You want to know how to get you sixty sacks?"

"How's that?"

"Don't fool around."

"You telling me I wasn't working as hard as any man in that field?"

"I don't know what you was doing out there, but them onions wasn't putting up no fight against me.

Driver, what you waiting on? I didn't come out here to look at no scenery."

They were driven to a labor camp enclosed by a high Cyclone fence topped with barbed wire, and as the crew rose to join the pay line outside, the driver blocked the way. "Now I want each and every one of those onion knives. I want you to file out one by one and I want every one of those knives."

"You going look like a pincushion," said the sixty-sack Negro.

The crew handed over the short, wooden-handled knives, and the driver frowned under the exertions of authority. "One by one, one by one," he repeated, though the aisle was too narrow for departing otherwise.

Tully stepped down into the dust and felt the sun again on his burned neck. Standing in the pay line behind the old man, he looked down the rows of white-washed barracks. A pair of stooped men in loose trousers, and shirts darkened down the backs with sweat, passed between buildings. In the brief swing of a screen door Tully saw rows of iron bunks. A Mexican with both eyes blackened crossed the yard carrying a towel. Tully moved ahead in the line. The paid were leaving the window of the shack and returning to the bus, some lining up again at a water faucet.

"Is that all you picked?" the paymaster demanded of the old man. "What's the matter with you, Pop? If you can't do better than that tomorrow I'm going to climb all over you."

"Well, it takes a while to get the hang of it," came the grieving reply.

Two dimes were laid on the counter under the open window. "Here's your money."

The old man waited. "Huh?"

"That's it."

The creased neck sagged further forward. Slowly the blackened fingers, the crustaceous nails, picked up the dimes. The slack body showed just the slightest inclination toward departing, though the split shoes, the sockless feet, did not move, and at that barely discernible impulse toward surrender, three one-dollar bills were dealt out. With a look of baffled resignation the man slouched away, giving place to Billy Tully, who stepped up to the grinning paymaster with his tally card.

As the bus passed out through the gate, Tully saw, nailed on a whitewashed wall, a yellow poster.

BOXING

ESCOBAR

VASQUEZ

The posters were up along Center Street when the bus unloaded in Stockton. There was one in the window of La Milpa, where Tully laid his five-dollar bill on the bar and drank two beers, eyeing the corpulent waitress under the turning fans, before taking the long walk to the lavatory. He washed his face, blew his dirt-filled nose in a paper towel, and combed his wet hair.

On El Dorado Street the posters were in windows of bars and barber shops and lobbies full of open-mouth dozers. Tully went to his room in the Roosevelt Hotel.

Tired and stiff but clean after a bath in a tub of cool gray water, he returned to the street dressed in a red sport shirt and vivid blue slacks the color of burning gas. Against the shaded wall of Square Deal Liquors, he joined a rank of leaners drinking from cans and pint bottles discreetly covered by paper bags. Across the street in Washington Square rested scores of men, prone, supine, sitting, some wearing coats in the June heat, their wasted bodies motionless on the grass. The sun slanted lower and lower through the trees, illuminating a pair of inert legs, a scabbed face, an outflung arm, while the shade of evening moved behind it, reclaiming the bodies until the farthest side of the park had fallen into shadow. Billy Tully crossed the sidewalk to the wire trash bin full of empty containers and dropped in his bottle. Over the town a dark haze of peat dust was blowing from the delta fields.

He ate fried hot dogs with rice in the Golden Gate Café, his shoes buried in discarded paper napkins, each stool down the long counter occupied, dishes clattering, waitresses shouting, the cadaverous Chinese cook, in hanging shirt and spotted khaki pants piled over unlaced tennis shoes, slicing pork knuckles, fat pork roast and tongue, making change with a greasy hand to the slap slap of the other cook's flyswatter.

Belching under the streetlights in the cooling air, Tully lingered with the crowds leaning against cars and parking meters before he went on to the Harbor Inn. Behind the bar, propped among the mirrored faces in that endless twilight was another poster. If Escobar can still do it so can I, Tully thought, but he felt he could not even get to the gym without his wife.

He felt the same yearning resentment as in his last months with her, the same mystified conviction of neglect.

At midnight he negotiated the stairs to his room, its walls covered with floral paper faded to the hues of old wedding bouquets. Undressing under the dim bulb, he stared at the four complimentary publications on the dresser: *An Hour With Your Bible. El Centenela y Heraldo de la Salud. Signs of the Times—The World's Prophetic Monthly. Smoke Signals—A Renowned Anthropologist Marshals the Facts on What Smoking Does to Life Before Birth.* He wondered if anyone ever read them. Maybe old men did, and wetbacks staying in off the streets at night. And was this where he was going to grow old? Would it all end in a room like this? He sat down on the bed and before him on the wall was the picture of the wolf standing with vaporized breath on a snow-covered hill above a lighted farm. Then the abeyant melancholy of the evening came over him. He sat with his shoulders slumped under the oppression of the room, under the impasse that was himself, the utter, hopeless thwarting that was his blood and bones and flesh. Afraid of a crisis beyond his capacity, he held himself in, his body absolutely still in the passing and fading whine and rumble of a truck. The blue and gold frame, the long cord hanging from the molding, the discolored gold tassel at its apex, all added to the feeling that he had seen the picture in some room in childhood. Though it filled him with despondency he did not think of taking it down, or of throwing out the maga-

zines and pamphlets and removing from the door
the sign

IF YOU SMOKE IN BED

PLEASE LET US KNOW

WHERE TO SEND YOUR ASHES.

It did not occur to him that he could, because he did
not even feel he lived here.

In the dark he arranged himself with tactical facility
in the lumpy terrain of the mattress. When the pounding came again on the door, he lunged up in the blackness crying: "Help!"

Out in the hall the hoarse voice warned: "Four
o'clock."

IO

Confidence, Ruben Luna believed, was the indispensable ingredient of success, and he had it in abundance —as much faith in his destiny as in the athletes he trained. In his own years of battling he had had doubts which at times became periods of terror. With a broken jaw wired into silence, he had sucked liquid meals through a tube, wondering if he were even sane. After a severe body beating and a bloody urination in the dressing room, he had wondered if the big fights and large sums he had thought would be coming but never came could be worth what he had already endured. But now Ruben's will was like a pure and unwavering light that burned even in his sleep. It was more a fatalistic optimism than determination, and though he was not immune to anxiety over his boxers, he felt he was immune to despair. Limited no longer by his own capacities, he had an odds advantage that he had never had as a competitor. He knew he could last. But his fighters were less dependable. Some trained one day and laid off two, fought once and quit, lost their timing, came back, struggled into condition, gasped and missed and were beaten, or won several bouts and got married, or moved, or were drafted, joined the navy or went to jail, were bleeders, suffered headaches, saw double or broke their hands. There had been so many who found they were not fighters at all, and there were others who without explanation had simply ceased to appear at the gym and were never seen or heard about again by Ruben, though once in a while a forgotten face returned briefly in a dream and he went on addressing instructions to it as though the intervening years had never been.

With a passive habitual smile, Ruben worked to suffuse them all with his own assurance. At times it was impossible for him to control the praise and predictions that issued from him like thanks, and he was aware of exaggerating; yet he felt a boxer needed someone who believed in him, and if it were true that confidence could win fights, then he could not be sure his overestimates were really that at all.

Guiding Ernie Munger down a long aisle in the Oakland Auditorium, Ruben felt a prescience of victory. Ernie had won his last three fights—by decisions in Watsonville and Santa Cruz, by knockout in Modesto, where his opponent had been overcome as much by his own exertions as by Ernie's blows. Now under this great ceiling, in the midst of this large crowd at an annual event sponsored by the Oakland Police Department, Ruben no longer was fretting. He thought only of his posture, of maintaining his position beside Ernie, of the steps he was mounting to the ring, of the ropes he was then spreading, sitting on the middle strand as he raised the rope above for Ernie and Babe to duck under. As he bustled, administered and directed, he was functioning at his best and he felt again the soaring, yet controlled, excited wholeness, periodically his, that he thought of as his true self. Smiling, he dabbed at Ernie's brows and stroked a Vaseline stripe down his broad dented nose, regretting its disfigurement though believing that it was just as well for Ernie to start his career with the nose he was sure to have ended with anyway. At least he would not be preoccupied with protecting it.

At the bell, Ruben was standing behind Ernie just outside the ropes, facing a short Negro with bulging arms and a Mohawk haircut. Then, sitting on the ring steps beside Babe, their heads on the level of Ernie's dancing feet, Ernie's new gold-trimmed white robe still over his arm, Ruben experienced the first waning of confidence. He saw in the Negro's opening blow a power that was undeniable, that was extraordinary. It was a wide hook slung to the stomach under Ernie's jab; and as instantaneous strategic adjustments were occurring in Ruben's mind, Ernie was struck under the heart with a right of resounding force. Ruben then felt a foreboding. Though Ernie maneuvered with a degree of skill, there was an aspect of futility in it all. When he reached out with both gloves to block a left, Ruben's hand went into his sweater pocket for the ammonia vial and a right swing landed with an awesome slam on the lean point of Ernie's chin. He went down sideways along the ropes, toppling stiffly in the roar, and hit the canvas on his back, his head striking the floor, followed by his feet. His eyes stared momentarily, then closed as his body went rigid.

Ruben was on the apron cutting Ernie's shoelaces with surgical scissors when the count began. But the referee did not complete it. He signified the obvious with a wave of his arms and bent down to remove the mouthpiece. Ruben left the shoes, ducked into the ring, cut the laces of the gloves and jerked the gloves off. He was on his knees cutting away the handwraps when the ringside doctor came through the ropes. The doctor pulled up his trousers and squatted. With a long pale index finger he lifted one lid and then another from the brown motionless eyes that gazed sightlessly up at the circle of faces. Hands shaking, Ruben waved the ammonia vial under the dented nose. Babe, pressing a chunk of ice against the nape of Ernie's neck, pulled his ears, and the referee stretched the gold waistband up from Ernie's abdomen as it heaved in desperately rapid respiration.

A minute must have gone by. The Negro, in his green robe now, came and stood with his seconds over the prostrate form, and still Ernie had not moved. His legs had quivered for an instant after he had fallen, and that had frightened Ruben as much as the rigidness that followed. He was clear of blame, but he was terrified. He felt the same vertigo he had felt several years before when Jaime Guzman collapsed in the gym. He had not been clear then, and he had suffered the remorse of one warned a hundred times yet who had persisted. Barely able to stand, he had told solemn doctors and indifferent hospital attendants about the protective headguard and the sixteen ounces of padding in each glove, of how Guzman had got up after the knockdown and even shadowboxed before going to the locker room. He repeated it all to Guzman's crying wife in the waiting room, and after Guzman died in surgery he explained it to a reporter on the phone, naming the other man who had been in the ring, telling of the brief time Guzman had been in training, once more describing the knockdown and once more omitting the other that had come before it and omitting how he had chided him and made him go on despite the look he had seen briefly in his eyes, until he had gone down the second time and the look was clear to everybody in the gym. Ruben had felt he was finished then, but he had also speculated that Guzman might have been hurt in one of his bouts in the navy before he had come to him. In the gym after the funeral there was no mention of the other knockdown, and he devoted himself to the benefit fight that raised for the widow ten percent of a $1,600 gate. Gradually he overcame the memory of the face in the casket. With a toupee over the shaved skull, it had resembled no one he had ever known anyway. But now under the ring lights Ruben experienced the same dread, and as he massaged Ernie's arms with unhurried hands, his face distressed but not frantic, he felt the hopeless folly that was his life.

It lasted until Ernie's lids at last began to flutter. As his eyes opened, blinked, squinted and closed again, Ruben struggled to contain his joy, afraid it too was error.

"What's your name?" asked the doctor in an imperious tenor, and Ruben passed the ammonia again under Ernie's nose. This time there was a slight recoiling. "That's enough of that," said the doctor, but Ruben felt he was the superior in experience and moved the vial once more past the nostrils. Ernie grimaced. Twitching, blinking, he tried to raise his head.

"What's your name?"

Ernie squinted up at the faces.

"Where are you?"

"Did I get knocked out?"

"What's your name? Tell me what your name is. Can you do that?"

"Ernie Munger."

"What town are you in? Hum?"

"Oakland. What round is it?"

"It's all over. How many fingers do you see? Can you see my hand?"

When Ernie sat up, the Negro bent down to him for the belated gesture of sportsmanship, his face framed by a white towel. "Good fight. You all right now?"

Ernie looked at him dully. Babe rose, patted the victor's back and hoarsely whispered to his seconds: "Real good puncher."

Helped to his feet, Ernie stood with one shoulder hunched while Ruben and Babe tied the robe around him. His arms across their necks, his shoes gaping, he was conducted up the aisle and around a vendor shouting: "Cold beer!"

In the dressing room, Ruben held ice at the back of Ernie's neck, sending Buford Wills out for his fight accompanied only by Babe. "I'll be right out," he said.

"I'll catch up with you." He was conscious of the minutes going by as he roughly toweled Ernie's body, as he helped him on with his clothes, gave him a drink of brandy from the medical kit, studied his eyes and draped the robe over his shoulders as he sat shivering on the rubbing table. He heard the bell as he was taking his pulse. "How you feel now?"

"Head hurts. Can I have some water?"

Ruben heard the shouts of the crowd and felt the pull of the fight like a physical compulsion. He ran for another manager's water bottle, covered with grimy adhesive tape, and as he was returning with it, the door hurled open and Babe was in the room again, shouting inaudibly. "He's cut!" Ruben saw the lips say before the croaking sounds registered, and he ran to the medical kit. With the water bottle still in his other hand, he ran past Babe out into the cavernous auditorium, soaring with that grave yet turbulent completeness down the aisle toward the square of glaring light where Buford Wills, small and frail and black, with a trickle of blood down his face, was battling a tattooed Mexican.

II

Wearing a new straw hat, Billy Tully crawled for seven days in the onion fields, then he was back on the dark morning street among crowds of men left behind by the buses, acridly awake with nothing to do at the impossible hour of 5 a.m. The men grumbled about workers from Mexico, talked of the canneries hiring, passed bottles, knelt in doorways for furtive games of crap, and in the blue light of dawn dwindled away, up Main and Market, along Center and El Dorado, back to the hotels, the lawn and shade of Washington Square, to Chinese and Mexican cafés and to the bars whose doors again were opening.

After reading the paper over coffee and eggs, Tully went back to his room, slept awhile on top of the covers, then took a bus across town. In a crowd of several hundred he stood in the sweet-sour stench of stewing peaches outside a cannery. Trucks passed laden with peach lugs and can-filled cartons. On a vast paved area behind a Cyclone fence, yellow forklifts were stacking lugs into piles the size of barns. Amid the hum of machinery, gleaming empty cans clattered constantly down a conveyor from a boxcar where a man was unstacking and feeding them to the belt with a wooden pitchfork. Blocking the steps to the office, an aged watchman armed with a billy club and a large revolver, his pants hiked above his belly and dewlaps quivering over his buttoned and tieless collar, warned the crowd to keep back from the building.

"Are you hiring or not?" Tully demanded, sweating and irritable now that the sun had cleared the roof.

"You'll just have to wait and hear from them inside."

"It don't do them no good us standing here. Why can't they come out and say if they don't want us?"

"I wouldn't know nothing about that."

"Then let me go in and ask somebody."

"Keep back. No one's going in that office."

"Why not? Who the hell you think you're talking to?"

"I'm just doing what they told me. They told me don't let nobody in the office and nobody's going through that door as long as I'm here. It's none of my doing."

"They're hiring all right," said a man at Tully's side. "I was out here yesterday and they said come back today."

Tully pushed to the front of the crowd and stood with his hands on his hips to prevent anyone from pushing around him. One of the big corrugated steel doors was open; visible in the gloom of the cannery were lines of aproned women. Inside the doorway a forklift had set down a pallet stacked with full lugs, and now a man left the crowd, stepped into the doorway and came back with two peaches. Several men and women followed, returning with handfuls of fruit before the watchman arrived and took the peaches from one final, grinning, capitulating pilferer. At that moment two Negro women sat down on the office steps. The guard ran belligerently back, neck and pelvis forward, squared chin bony from the downward abandonment by its flesh. Arguing, the women rose, and his head turned from them to the open door, from which one more man slipped back to the crowd with a handful of peaches.

"Well, you old fart, are they hiring or not?" shouted Tully.

"Not your kind. You can go home right now."

A whistle blew, the cans stopped rolling from the boxcar, the women inside the building left the line, and the office door was opened by a youthful, sober-faced man in a white short-sleeve shirt with a striped tie.

"The cannery won't be hiring any more personnel at the present time," he announced from the porch. "We've got our full crews for peaches. Come back when the tomatoes are ripe."

A peach banged against the corrugated metal wall several yards to his side—a loud juiceless thump.

"Who did that?" shouted the watchman. He was answered with snickers. The man on the porch stated that throwing peaches would not get anybody a job, and he went back into the office. The crowd fragmented, people walking off down the sides of the street, some running to parked cars, some remaining in the yard as if not believing the announcement. Tully went over to the open cannery door.

"Not hiring!" yelled the watchman.

Nearby in the immense dim room, a girl in jeans and workshirt was seated on a pallet eating a sandwich, her neck round and sloping, with short black curls at the nape.

The watchman arrived wheezing. "Not hiring. Come back when the tomatoes are ripe. Don't take any of that fruit."

Tully took a peach and walked past him into the sunlight. The small chunk he managed to bite away he spit out. When he threw the peach against the front door of a house, it struck with the hardness of stone. Along the sides of the street green peaches lay in the weeds.

The next morning he went out with a busload of tomato thinners. It was a day haul he had many times been warned against, but it paid ninety cents an hour. There was no talk on the ride out of town. The men slept; those with seats to themselves lay down on them. By sunrise they were in the delta.

Preceded by another, the bus jolted down a dirt road to a field bordered by irrigation ditches. With a few groans but mostly in silence, the men climbed out into the sparkling air and selected short-handled hoes from the bed of a pickup truck. Then they jumped a ditch, a foreman already yelling on the other side, and they ranged over the field to continue the previous day's weeding. Bent double, chopping with hoes half a yard long, crossing and uncrossing their legs, they stepped sideways along the rows.

Tully glanced around, saw what was being done, and began chopping, trying to leave an isolated tomato plant every width of a hoe blade. Engulfed by new weeds, grass and dandelion, they were seedlings growing in a double line down each row.

"What the hell kind of weeding you call that?"

Tully turned to a pair of legs in clean khaki. Straightening, he confronted a black mustache on a face he assumed, from its displeasure, was a foreman's. Then he turned to the ground he had cleared: long, leafless gaps, interrupted by infrequent plants, several of which appeared now not to be tomatoes.

"Shape up and get your ass in gear or you can spend the day in the bus."

"Tough shit. A lot I care. Big deal," Tully whispered at the departing back, wanting to hurl his hoe at it. He stooped lower, gripped the handle closer to the blade and hacked on. Instead of spaced plants, for a yard of mounting anxiety he left nothing at all. Sliding his hand all the way down to the blade, he meticulously scraped around the next plant, cutting down grass and weeds in a closer and closer square, plucking with his free hand until the tomato with its two jagged leaves and an adjacent red-rooted weed stood alone; and then in one final minuscule nick both were down. Guiltily, he peered around before propping the tomato plant upright between two clods. Already his back was hurting. The pain began at his waist, spread down the backs of his thighs to the tendons behind the knee joints and up the spine to the shoulders and the back of the neck. A tractor came up his row pulling a disk harrow, and when Tully straightened and moved aside for it to roar past, plowing under the chopped weeds, tiny transparent specks quivered before his eyes. He was falling behind. Soon he was the last stooped man moving across the field, and the foreman, stepping in long strides over the rows, again came threatening dismissal. Tully chopped on with desperate imprecision, dismayed by the lowness of the sun, which seemed to hang stationary. He doubted his back could last, and it was not the loss of the money, a day-long wait or the hitchhiking back he feared. It was the disgrace, for all around him were oaths, moans, bellowed complaints, the brief tableaux of upright wincing men, hoes dangling, their hands on the small of their backs, who were going on under the same torment—some of them winos, donut and coffee men, chain smokers, white-bread eaters, maybe none ever athletes yet all moving steadily on while he fell farther and farther behind, hacking in panic over the desertion of his will. He could not resign himself to the inexorable day; he would have to quit, and the others, he felt, were fools in their enduring. Including himself, only three men out of two busloads were white.

He could resolve no more than to clear the next six inches before throwing down his hoe. He straightened up with difficulty and stared hazily at the blue sky that was scrawled with the familiar floating patterns etched for so long now on his eyes. He breathed deeply, stretched, bent back over the row, crouched, knelt, crawled, scrambled up, and all the while the ache in his back continued. He lasted until noon, until the unbelievable half hour of relief. Ten minutes of it he spent waiting in line at a pickup truck to buy bean and potato filled tortillas and a Pepsi-Cola.

"Jesus Christ, you don't care where you eat, do you?" asked one of the two white men passing him where he lay under a pepper tree among a humming profusion of green-glinting flies whose source of delight, he noticed now, lay directly beside him. He had thought the odor was coming from his lunch. With a twinge of embarrassment he rose and entered a bus—sweltering and full of Negroes—and sat next to a man reeking of Sloan's liniment.

Tully was falling asleep while he finished eating, but already the men were hobbling out of the bus and taking up their hoes. Following, he found himself off with the Negroes at one end of the field. Bloated, aching, he again bent over a row. Shuffling sideways, his legs crossing and uncrossing, the short hoe rising and falling, he labored on in the despondency of one condemned, the instrument of his torture held in his own hand. Of all the hated work he had ever done, this was a torment beyond any, almost beyond belief, and so it began to seem this was his future, that this was Work, which he had always tried to evade and would never escape now that his wife was gone and his career was over. And it was as if it were just, as if he deserved no better for the mess he had made of his life. Yet he also felt he could not go on even another hour. He felt his existence had come to a final halt, with no way open to him anywhere. Hand on his back, straightening, he gazed with bleary eyes at all the stooped men inching down the rows, and he felt being white no longer made any difference. His life was being swept in among those countless lives lost hour by captive hour scratching at the miserable earth.

"You call this a living?"

"Uh hum," responded the man he had lunched beside, who, though young, appeared to have lost all his teeth and whose scent of liniment was periodically wafted to Tully's nose.

"How long's it take to get use to this shit, anyway?" Tully asked, and was nettled by gleeful forlorn laughter from the chopping and shuffling men.

"What a man want, what a man *need*, is a woman with a good job."

"I had that," Tully said. "But she left."

Again there was that irritating laughter. Tully hoed on in silence, listening to a bantering discussion of divorce, which everyone around him seemed to have undergone.

The wind came up; some of the men across the field masked themselves with bandannas, like bandits, and those who had come with goggles around the crowns of their straw hats drew them over their eyes. The peat dust blew in trails across the field and the blue of the sky was obscured by a gray haze through which the sun shone dully like the lid of a can. Tully forced himself on and the others drew steadily away. Dizzy, the tendons at the back of his knee joints swollen and stiff, he stood upright, watching the foreman. He stumbled across the clods to the water can on the back of a jeep that moved slowly up the rows and idled among the men, and he drank a long time from the sticky tin cup. Rebuked for lingering, he limped back cursing. Even his eyes ached in the downward strain of stooping. He trailed farther and farther behind, the Negroes' voices growing faint, blown by the wind.

The sun sloped down the sky, the bent men moved on across the black earth. Tully was hardly thinking now, his mind fixed on pain and chopping and a vision of quitting time. Seeing a man go to the edge of the field, he rose and went to the foreman, who was suspicious but gave his permission. In the tall grass beside an irrigation ditch, Tully squatted a peaceful moment.

When a white sedan arrived, raising a long trail of dust, Tully was lying in the dirt, propped on one arm, doggedly chopping. He did not understand that its appearance signified the end of the day until some of the crew began leaping over the rows and incredibly racing to the car, where a man now stood at the fender with a small green strongbox.

"Who wants to make a store stop?" the driver asked on the road back to Stockton. So empty cans and bottles clanked along the floor when the bus arrived with its silent motionless passengers in the sunlit town.

"You'll never see me again," declared Tully, and he swayed, leaning oddly backwards, up the street to his hotel, straw cowboy hat cocked forward, his fingers discovering new mounds of muscle in the small of his agonized back.

But the pay was ninety cents an hour, and two days later he was again gripping a short-handled hoe.

12

I'm getting my share, Ernie Munger assured himself at the station on Center Street under floodlights besieged by moths. Still he felt an uneasiness, an indefinable lack. He would phone Faye, talking on sometimes after a car crossed the thin black hose between office and pumps, talking while it waited, and complaining at the departing ring that the customer had not given him a chance to get out there.

"Are you very busy tonight?" Faye would ask, and he, thinking he heard an impinging, possessive, matrimonial tone, would feel a deadening resentment. Other times her voice was cheerfully independent and he felt he was in love.

On his nights off, his arm around her in a movie, he waited impatiently for the evening's consummation in the car. But at its approach she became somber, and afterwards was tense, petulant, glum.

"What's the matter?" he asked late one night on a levee amid sounds of crickets and frogs and the close rustle of leaves.

"Nothing."

In the distance, dominating the lights of the town, the red neon crest of Stockton's twelve-story skyscraper flashed, a line at a time.

CALIFORNIA

WESTERN

STATES

LIFE

PROTECTION

"Don't you feel good?"

"I'm all right."

"Is anything wrong?"

"I said *nothing.*"

"Well, what you getting mad about then?"

"I'm not *mad.*"

"Okay."

"Can't I be quiet if I feel like it without everybody getting all worked up?"

"You're the only one getting worked up."

"Well, leave me alone then. I have a right to my moods."

"All right, I can take a hint. Don't think I don't know what's wrong. I'm not stupid. I know what it is. Maybe you need somebody that's got more to give you."

"That's not it."

"You're unfulfilled. I know, I'm sorry, I'm not blind."

"I'm fulfilled. I'm perfectly fulfilled. That's not it at all."

"You didn't get real fulfillment."

"I feel perfectly fine. I'm fulfilled. Now don't worry

about it. That's not what's bothering me at all. I just feel out of touch sometimes."

"You mean you're mad."

"I'm not mad. I'm a little worried, that's all."

Ernie felt a dismal apprehension. "What about?"

"You know what."

"We've been pretty careful."

"You've been pretty careful. If I was careful I'd never come out here. You wouldn't marry me now, I know you wouldn't. Men just don't after they've slept with somebody."

"They do too. They do it all the time. What are you talking about?"

"You wouldn't."

Caught between prudence and expediency, afraid of committing himself and afraid of losing his rights to her, he replied despondently: "I would too."

"When?"

"Well, when it's right for us both. We don't want to rush into a mess when we've got each other anyway."

"Don't you want to be with me every night?"

"Sure I do. Maybe I could get a day job."

"That's not what I meant."

"I guess I don't feel ready yet. I feel I need a few more fights first," he heard himself saying. "I just don't feel I'm ready to get married."

"I wasn't proposing to you. That's a thing I certainly would never do. I wouldn't want anybody who didn't want me."

"I want you."

"That's up to you. I wouldn't force myself on anyone. If you don't want to get married you don't have to. I wasn't asking anything about that. I just meant what if, you know, you got drafted or something—how do I know where I stand? Would you want me to wait?"

"Well, sure," said Ernie, thinking there was no harm in that and piqued by the thought of someone else having her.

"I mean these are things I'm just asking for my own sake. I don't want you to feel I'm obligating you."

"I don't, I don't," he assured her.

"Like what would you want if you had some more fights? What's that got to do with it? Would that make a difference? What would you feel like doing after you had them?"

"Then I guess I'd want somebody so it'd seem worth getting my ass kicked . . . so I could . . . I don't know . . . have a home. But I want to get set up first," he said, unconvinced, afraid of what he was saying.

"I don't want to hold you back. I want to be good for you." She put her fingers on his cheek, her eyes only hollows in the dim starlight. "I want to cook for you."

It filled him with panic. To such devotion, such sacrifice, he felt rejection would be unbearable, that to quibble at all would be an unthinkable cruelty. Profoundly moved, he kissed the lax waiting mouth with exquisite unhappiness.

Later, on her front porch, she looked so lovely to him, so graceful, her full lips in a smile so gentle, that he could not turn and go home. So many obstacles, so much uncertainty lay ahead in consequence of what he had been forced to say in the car, that this time of intimacy had a transitory sweetness. He would not marry her, and so she would not be his much longer. Eventually there would be conditions he could not agree to. He must cherish the present like a memory. This would be the time of Faye, this would soon be over. Her presence, her voice, the taste of her mouth would be replaced by another's and lost forever. Or perhaps there would be no other after her and he would again be alone with his lust. He would not marry her, so felt a blissful freeing of his love, an elation that carried him after her through the doorway to a final kiss that became not the last but the first in a fevered goodbye with her skirt up and his little tin box out in the glove compartment of the car. Sitting on the carpeted stairs leading up to the room where he hoped her parents were asleep, he pulled her down onto his lap.

Afterwards Ernie was pensive. Through days of peat-dust storms he waited uneasily. When a month was up he drove Faye to a doctor and sat in the car knowing already what the answer would be and feeling a singular peace. He would quit fighting. Certainly now he could no longer take the risks. There was no decision to make. He had no thoughts of escape from her and was strangely unperturbed. There seemed to him only one thing to do. They were married in the Little Chapel of the Wayfarer in Carmel, the bride wearing a white dress, the groom expressionless in sport coat and slacks. After a dinner of swordfish steak on the wharf in Monterey, they phoned the news to their parents and rented a motel room under cypress trees. Two nights later they were sleeping in Faye's room.

On Ernie's second night back at work, his employer, Mario Florestano, was waiting for him in the doorway of the station, the largeness of his alerted face accentuated by frontal baldness, long ears, a slight neck and narrow shoulders.

"You left the shitter open," he said.

Ernie, seeking an attitude, looked at him with puzzled eyes. "I did? I thought I locked it up."

"You certainly did not. Want me to tell you what I saw when I drove in this morning? A wino coming out putting toilet paper in his pocket."

"I'd swear I locked it."

"Listen, didn't you hear me? I said I saw him coming *out*. Now what I want to know is how he got in."

"I can't figure it." Ernie gravely pulled on the end of his nose. "I'd swear I remember checking the door before I left."

"You couldn't of checked that door. That door was open. How else did he get in there and get that toilet paper? Did he have a passkey?"

"I don't know, he might of had one. I sure don't remember leaving that door open."

"Forget it, forget I ever said anything about it. Don't go on any more. It's settled." Florestano paced off under dangling fan belts, turned abruptly and came back. "If you don't want to admit it, forget it. He got in there and he got the toilet paper and arguing won't bring it back. Now I'm not trying to accuse you if you don't want to admit it. I just want you to realize your mistake so it won't happen again."

"I'd admit it if I thought I did it."

"I'm sure you would."

"If you want to put the blame on me it's up to you."

"No, no, it's not a matter of blaming anyone. These things happen. It was just something I wanted to call your attention to. Nobody wants to sit on a toilet seat a wino's been on. It's like shaking your dick where a nigger shook his. You got to think of the public. It's public relations. Personally I couldn't care less. One man's as good as another as long as they pay their way. Only there's people around that don't feel that way. So if an undesirable asks you for the key, the shitter's out of order. It's just a matter of consideration. If there's no undesirable piss on the toilet seat you'll get repeat customers. So that door stays locked."

"I *keep* it locked."

Mario Florestano gave him a long look. "So how's married life treating you?"

Left in charge, Ernie scattered sawdust on the floor of the lube room, pushed it around with a long-handled broom, scooped it up blackened, and dumped it in a drum of empty oil cans. He wiped off the grease rack, wiped and hung up the tools and ambled out to cars, thumbs hooked in his pants pockets. When the streetlights came on he went to the switchbox and the night air quivered in the tall white beams of the floodlights.

13

Along El Dorado and Center Streets between Mormon Slough and the deep-water channel hundreds of farm workers and unemployed loitered in the warm summer evenings. They talked, watched, drifted in and out of crowded bars and cardrooms, cafés, poolhalls, liquor stores and movies, their paths crossed by lines of urine from darkened doorways. Around the area cruised squad cars and patrol wagons with their pairs of peering faces. The fallen, the reeling and violent were conveyed away. Ambulances came driven by policemen. Fire trucks arrived and sodden, smoking mattresses were dragged out to the pavement. Evangelists came with small brass bands. Sometimes a corpse was taken down from a hotel. Occasionally in *The Stockton Record* there was an editorial deploring blight.

On the morning the orange city maintenance trucks came to Washington Square, Billy Tully was sitting on the grass. The park was a block of lawn and shade trees within a periphery of tall date palms with high sparse fronds, faced on one side by the ornate eaves of Confucius Hall and on the opposite side by the slate steeple and red brick of Saint Mary's Church.

"Now what they going to do, mow the grass?" he said after the three vehicles had parked and the workmen were climbing down from the cabs.

"Pick up trash, I guess," said a tanned, wrinkled man sitting near him in the shade.

Chains rattled, tailgates dropped, tools were dragged over truckbeds. The workmen entered the park with axes and chain saws.

"Must be a diseased tree," said Tully, and a man with a scab down the bridge of his nose announced: "Tree surgeons. Probably a diseased tree."

The last day haul had departed for the fields hours before. There were perhaps forty men reclining on the grass—gaunt night sleepers in coats, and farm workers in shirt sleeves, unhired at the morning shape-up. Two men and a woman in overalls rose from under the tree where the workmen stopped.

"Tree surgeons," shouted the man with the scab after the rope starter had been pulled on the first chain saw. Roaring and sputtering like an outboard motor, the saw dug into the tree. In a moment another saw was roaring on the other side of the park. Ropes were thrown up into the foliage, sawdust flew, the trees swayed, tilted over, cracking, and fell with a rush of green leaves and a crash of branches. Men were rising, shambling away, and one after another the trees they had rested under came crashing down. Billy Tully remained propped up on his elbows, his legs flat on the lawn, until the crew reached his tree. He got up with the others, everyone surly and argumentative, walking away while a workman called after them.

"Hey, move your buddy."

An inert man remained behind unresponsive to prodding feet.

"He's no buddy of mine," said Tully.

"He won't be anybody's buddy if he don't move."

"That's your problem."

"He's breathing," said the other workman.

The man was lifted up at the knees and shoulders, head hanging sideways, mouth open, sockless ankles and thin white shins dangling. He was pulled in opposite directions, his legs were dropped, he was dragged on his rear as the man holding him at the armpits stumbled backward. Again he lay on his back. Exchanging accusations, the two workmen once again grasped the slack limbs and carried him out of the shade.

Tully went back to the heat of his room. Barefoot and shirtless on the bed, he read a *Male* magazine and dozed to the sound of the saws a block away. They roared all day. By mid-afternoon, when returning laborers were arriving from the farms and Tully strolled back to the park, all the shade trees were down. Many of the trunks had been cut into sections and much of the foliage was gone. Across the park, as on the days that followed—when the trunks and limbs and stumps had all been cleared away and the patches of bare earth seeded—men lay lined in the elongated shadows of the palms and out in the glare of the sun.

14

Ernie and Faye Munger moved into three rooms on the ground floor of an old, three-story, white shingle apartment house. The kitchen faced onto garbage cans and lawn chairs in a back yard enclosed by a hedge, and dishes occasionally vibrated in the cabinet from a motor idling in a garage beyond the wall. Faye's mother, perpetually smiling and exclaiming, her green eyes wide open and fearful, came and hung curtains. She treated Ernie with an awkward deference, her disappointment evident in sidelong looks, and he spoke to her in a polite son-in-law cant intended to convince her of his exceptional qualities.

In the curtained shadows he slept late, waking to find Faye, often nauseous, already up and dressed, his mornings not the times of sensual indolence he had imagined. At night he phoned the apartment from the station, and if Faye did not answer he called her parents' house, where he invariably reached her, the ensuing conversations interrupted by customers, the receiver left on the desk while he slopped a wet rag over windshields, decided if a deficiency of oil was worth mentioning, peered into radiators but left the filling of them for another time and place. By the time he had locked up and driven home, Faye was usually asleep. They made love in the heat of the day.

Often they were visited by Faye's friend, Norma Panelli, who discussed with Faye in the kitchen the fortunes of various couples, the girls' voices at times sinking to whispers. To Norma Ernie spoke little, in order to discourage too soon a return.

With Faye crushed against him, he drove between the flat hot fields to Lodi or Tracy or Modesto, where they turned around to come back. He threw her into Oak Park Pool, swam to her underwater with lascivious fingers, stood on his hands with only his long white feet above the surface, ran off the high board and belly-flopped from the low, and with eyes stinging from chlorine, lay down panting beside her on the hot wet cement. When she walked between the pool and the dressing room his was not the only head that turned to watch. Coming home from these swims he was often ill-tempered and taciturn. One afternoon a car cut in front of them, the driver looking back as Ernie, brandishing a middle finger, filled the intersection with curses.

"You better be careful," Faye warned.

"Careful of him? He's just a sack of shit!"

"Stop doing that! He's liable to see you."

"I want him to see it! He's the one better be careful."

In the apartment, Ernie continued to brood over the incident, wondering: who does she think she married? And it seemed that she neither knew nor respected him, that she denied the very basis of his personality.

By the next day the occurrence had lost its significance. She was a girl, after all, and could have no sure sense of who he was. He forgave her, for that incomprehension itself attested to the uncommonness of his kind. It was enough that she love the part of him she knew; the other needed nothing from anybody. I don't give a rat's ass, was his motto. It was not comprehension he wanted, only her awareness that he was not like anyone she had known before. But it was as if what distinguished him was what she did not perceive. At times as he lay in bed listening to her breathing, a fear came over him that after marriage death was the next major event.

Sometimes he was euphoric; he rewarded her with bouts of ardor, gaining energy as hers was depleted. At meals he jiggled his legs. In the midst of a conversation he might suddenly drop to the floor and begin doing pushups.

"You're the most nervous guy," Faye said as Ernie was absorbed in rolling his neck while thoroughly masticating a raw carrot. "When you relax you really relax, but when you're just sitting around you're always moving."

"I'm exercising," he stated through the uproar in his jaws. "Most people neglect their necks."

"I don't mean just that. Look how you're chewing."

"That's how to get the most out of a carrot."

He was stimulated, he was pleased, yet at times he gazed at her for long moments, as if to gain by concentration some final elusive dominion. He would reach out and fondle her, amazed still at the breadth of his license. He buried his face in her, explored, examined, turned her about. I've liberated her, he told himself, yet was sometimes assailed by a strange sickening excitement and wondered if it were he who deserved the credit.

"I don't want anybody but you," he declared.

"I don't ever want anybody but you," she responded. But Ernie felt no different. "I really mean it."

"I do too."

"I mean I never will."

"Me neither."

But he wondered if she would have said it without his saying it first. Often she told him she loved him, but that was not enough, even if it were true. She must have loved others before him, and where were they now? She had married him, but had there been any choice? What if she had never met him? Would it all have happened the same way with somebody else? When she amused herself one day with his hair, parting it and combing the sides down instead of upward and back, he felt he was not the man she wanted, and respected her less for her taste.

Alone in the bedroom he shadowboxed before the mirror, but with no desire to return to the gym. All that seemed impossible now; there was not enough time in a day. Though he was up for hours before going to work, still he was usually late, because he could not leave Faye until the moment when he had to leave in frantic haste.

He was broody, he was amorous. While reading, he noticed a minute blizzard falling before his eyes and found himself massaging his scalp in a frenzy. He fell asleep with leaps and twitches and dreamed of being rushed off unprepared for a bout he had forgotten. He saw no one from the Lido Gym, and Ruben Luna never phoned, as Ernie had feared he would. A sense of safety, comfort, luxury, took possession of him. Only to be with Faye, to work, sleep and make love was like a reprieve, an indulgence. At times he wondered if he were losing his nerve.

When Faye bathed, he soaped her with a sense of privilege. Drying her off, he caressed her in admiration. Her short sturdy body showed no sign of pregnancy; her belly was flat except for a tilting of pelvis, a slightly rearward slope from the navel to the tuft of black hair. "You're in great shape," he said. "Only you're wide open." And squaring off, he tapped her belly. At first she responded with a tolerant smile, soon with impatience, and once with the cry: "Don't," her hands at her sides, her heavy breasts, nipples dark and thick, hanging incongruously before his poised fists. Hurt, he turned away thinking she had no sense of humor. That she was already growing bored with him seemed indicated by her occasional disinclination for the daily sexual regimen. He wondered if he was adequate to her needs. One day he did two hundred consecutive sit-ups.

The summer passed in waves of worry and concupiscence, until Faye took employment with the Pacific Gas and Electric Company. Ernie then slept later than ever, ate breakfast with his jaw propped in his palm, and looked out the kitchen window at oiled female neighbors lying back in the lawn chairs, their crying babies filling him with dread. He went out to his Ford and drove along the hot streets.

One day at Dick's Drive-Inn he walked over to a low maroon car. Slumped behind the wheel, his wan pinched face barely above the door, sat Gene Simms.

"What say, man?"

"What's happening?"

"Nothing. Where you been keeping yourself?"

"Around. What's new?"

"Nothing."

Gene Simms was working nights at the box factory, and the two began passing afternoons together. Driving his car or riding in Ernie's, haggard, frowning, yawning, smoking with yellowed unsteady fingers, a blond oily lock hanging over his forehead, Gene talked mostly on the same subject, his descriptive powers arousing in Ernie a curious agitation and a fear that what he had with Faye might be of a quality below the possible or even the usual.

"There isn't a one that don't want it," said Gene.

"Well, I don't know."

"But you got to know what you're doing."

"That's right, sure, they won't go for just anybody."

"If the right guy comes along he can score."

"Everybody's got a mate somewhere."

"I don't care who it is. You know Eleanor MacDonald? I plugged her."

"I know, you told me."

"You got to understand their minds. If you can get your knee between their legs you're usually on your way."

Home from work in the first hours of morning, Ernie tried not to wake Faye, knowing she needed rest. Slowly he slid into bed, and as she turned to him he slipped his arm about her neck. Until she quieted he stroked her back or hair, her leg if it had fallen over him, then as her breathing settled he held her against him with a protectiveness so tender he was saddened because she was not awake to perceive it.

One afternoon, cruising Main Street with Gene Simms, he saw standing on a corner at parade rest a swarthy soldier in khakis and boots.

"By God, that's Bonomo," said Gene, who then yelled: "Bonomo, Bonomo! Hey, man, when'd you get back?" while Ernie drove on without a sideways glance. "Hey, stop, stop, that's Bonomo. He must be on leave. Stop, for Christ's sake. Hey, why didn't you stop, man? What's the matter?"

"Who the hell are you giving orders to? If you want to get out you can jump out."

"Well, let's go back. That was Bonomo."

"So it was Bonomo."

"Why didn't you stop?"

"Because I don't want to stop, that's why."

"Why not?"

"I said I don't want to!"

Whether Gene understood then or remembered something Ernie did not even know, or whether simply the vigor of that bellow proved conclusive, the subject abruptly ended. In the days that followed, Ernie avoided him, and that night he did not take Faye into his arms.

He lay apart from her in anguish at her faithlessness. If with Bonomo why not with others? Was Bonomo any better than anybody else? Ernie could conceive of no one worse. He was sick with murderous despair over the liberties that had been taken with his wife. Reminding himself that it had happened before she had known him made not the slightest difference, and telling himself that maybe nothing had happened was of no use. His first interest in Faye had come at seeing her riding along Main Street pressed against Bonomo, who was not known for wasting his time.

When she sprawled against Ernie, he recoiled, and at last he fell asleep clinging to the edge of the mattress.

For days he was churlish, agitated, glum. One night he woke with a jerk.

"Ernie, what's wrong?"

"Nightmare."

"What a pitiful noise you made."

"Had a nightmare."

"Poor Ernie, what was it?"

"Nothing."

"Was something after you?"

"What do you care?"

"Was it about me? Is that it?"

"You were in it. Leave me alone. It wasn't anything."

"Did I do something wrong? I can't help it if I did. I mean because I didn't really do anything."

"Didn't you?"

"No, I didn't. What was it?"

"It wasn't anything. Somebody came up and took your hand, that's all."

"Just that? Was that all?"

"And you let him."

"It was your dream. Don't blame me. Was it just that?"

"Isn't that enough? You did it right in front of me."

"Well, that isn't so bad. Maybe he was my father."

"He wasn't your father."

"Did he look like him?"

"You know who he was."

"I don't!"

"You sure?"

"I don't, I don't." She sat up, turned on the bedside lamp and looked down at him in alarm. "I didn't do anything."

"I'll bet you didn't."

"Ernie, it was just a dream. It isn't real, it didn't really happen."

"Didn't it?"

"I don't understand you. I didn't do that and I wouldn't and I don't see why you're making such a big fuss about it."

"What if it was Bonomo?"

"Was it him?"

Ernie nodded, watching her eyes.

"I'm sorry, but I mean it's not my fault. You know I went with him. You went with other girls, too."

"I know. Don't get the idea I'm jealous. I'm not. I just don't see why you couldn't find something better than that son-of-a-bitch."

"I did. I found you."

"Oh, come off it. What if he hadn't joined the army?"

"I wouldn't be with him. I never liked him."

"That just makes it worse. How many other guys didn't you like?"

"What do you mean?"

"Jesus, that's really something."

"What is?"

"Just that."

"Not liking him?"

"And letting him have you."

He saw fear in the gray evasive eyes. She was wearing a pale-blue nightgown and her hand rose to the ribbon threaded through the lace of the neck, then to her hair, the short fingers twisting a dark lock level with her chin.

"I didn't do that."

"You can tell me the truth. I know how it is. I accept that. It's only human. It's a natural drive. I don't hold it against you. But why with that rotten bastard? There ought to have been something else available, and I guess there was, too, wasn't there? It's only natural with a woman and I accept that. It really doesn't bother me. That's just the way things go. How can you fight nature? What's past is past. It's just the present that counts. But if I ever catch you with him I'll kill both of you."

"Who?"

"With anybody! I know what you were doing before you met me. It didn't take any great brain to figure that out."

"I didn't do anything."

"You don't have to lie to me. Tell me all about it, I don't care. It's natural enough—you're a healthy girl. I'm not jealous, I'm just warning you. Now okay, forget it, I'm not mad, everything's fine. For Christ's sake, don't cry. I'm not mad. What went on before me is your own business, and if anybody wises off I'll bust his head. Didn't you know he'd shoot his mouth off to everybody? Didn't you even think about that? That's what I can't stand—knowing that son-of-a-bitch is laughing about it. I'm going to kick ass royal around this shit town. Will you stop crying? I told you I'm not mad. Can't you understand that? Maybe you loved him, I don't know, though I don't see how you could, but maybe you did. I know you got urges. It wouldn't be right if you didn't."

She uttered a wail of such resonant grief, loud and deep like an inhuman moan, that he was frightened.

"Faye?"

She was silently rocking. From between her fingers tears dropped to the sheet. Again that deep animal moaning, terrifying in its immodesty, rose from behind her hands. It was a sound he had never heard before. He sat up, rigid, staring at her bowed head, her clenched and digging fingers, saying: "Faye, it doesn't bother me, it doesn't bother me. It really doesn't bother me. Faye, it doesn't bother me at all. It really doesn't bother me."

15

"Do you have any idea what it's like to be without that man?"

"Uh," said Billy Tully.

"And he didn't mean it. He just gets so nervous. You don't know what you have to take when you're interracial. Every son-of-a-bitch on the street has to get a look at you. And Earl's really a peaceable man. He's even-tempered. He didn't hurt that guy and he didn't want to. Just a little nick on the back of the neck. He wouldn't any more try to assult somebody than you'd get up on that stool and try to fly. He couldn't. He's just not made that way. He's the sweetest-natured man in the world."

"He'll get out," said Tully, glancing at her in the mirror, her eyes darkly circled, nose dented, mouth bracketed with lines, her lips red and sorrowful and with a fullness, for an instant there beyond the reflected bottles, like the fullness of his wife's lips. He turned to her, but her face was down and her lips, blocked from his view by her mass of curly hair, could not be like his wife's because his wife would not have worn that hairdo. His wife had had taste, which had the effect of disqualifying the woman beside him. He turned back to his drink with a pleasurably melancholy sense of fidelity. Impressed by the breadth of his love, he resigned himself. Hopefully he had come to sit by this woman, Oma, whom he remembered as having once intrigued him, but now he felt only indifference. As she talked on, he looked wearily down the lighted bar, lined with beer bottles, glasses, brown bare arms and hot-sauce bottles filled with salt. He had spent the day picking peaches.

"He's so jealous. I wouldn't put it past him to be out already, spying on every move I make."

Tully glanced at the open doorway. Mournful Mexican howls came from the jukebox. On a calendar above the ranks of Thunderbird and Silver Spur, a bare-breasted Aztec maiden lay sleeping at the feet of a warrior, flanked by two giant bottles of Cerveza XX, against a background of snow-capped volcanoes.

"He won't let me talk to people. He's so possessive. He'd never let me out of his sight. And he'd get so mad at me. You know when we talked last time, you and me, way back then? You know what he did to me afterwards? He raped me."

Tully turned to the brown eyes, the lids puffy, eyebrows a short stubble under bluish penciled lines.

"He just picked me up and threw me on the bed. Well, don't look at me like that. I'm not ashamed to say it. I've never been ashamed of the act of love. I believe it's a part of life."

Tully was regaining his interest. "Sure, why not? I mean, after all, if people like each other."

"I don't mean free love. I got no use for that."

"Well, free, depends what you mean free. If it's not free can you call it love?"

"I mean real love. I'm talking about love, not just sex. When you're really in love you marry for life. That's the only way it can be. I don't consider my second marriage sanctified. I should of stayed true to Frank."

"Who's that?"

"My first husband. He was a full-blooded Cherokee."

"You married an Indian?"

"What's wrong with that? You think you're any better?"

"I'm not knocking it."

"Just watch what you say. I won't stand for any insults against Frank. I heard enough smart talk when I married him. My family turned against me, and he was cleaner than any of them. They talk about Indians drinking. I never saw Frank drunk. I said to hell with all of them. He was the handsomest man I've ever known. I still wear his wedding ring."

Tully looked at the gold band. "What happened, you split up?"

"No."

"But you're not married any more."

Oma paused before replying: "I'm a widow."

He lowered his eyes. "Uh. Too bad. What happened to him?"

"He was shot."

"No kidding. Who did it?"

"He was a police officer. He was killed in the line of duty. He'd only been on the force two weeks and he didn't know what they do to you. He was too brave to be careful. A couple of guys were holding up a bar and he was right there, he and another officer. They got the call and they were right there before the men got off the sidewalk, and Frank jumped out of the car first and they killed him."

"Where was this?"

"Oakland. We moved up there after we got married and Frank worked in the post office, but that didn't pay enough and he didn't like it. Then he heard they needed policemen, and he was big. We didn't even have time to have children. I married white next time and all he was good for was running us off an embankment. Marrying him was the biggest mistake of my life. He had unnatural desires."

"He did?"

"The white race is in its decline. We started downhill in 1492 when Columbus discovered syphilis."

"What did he want to do?"

"White men are animals."

"We're not so bad."

"White man is the vermin of the earth!"

"All right, not so loud."

"Don't tell me what to do. Who do you think killed the American Indian? I don't care who hears me. I know I'm making a nuisance of myself to all these god-damn Mexicans sitting here just waiting for me to leave so they can get comfortable without any gringos around. To hell with these greaseballs. They don't know who their real friends are."

"What are you going on about? Take it easy."

"You can just shut your damn mouth. What do you know about it?"

"What did you say to me?"

"I said you can shut up. And keep your hands off me, too."

"What did you say? Listen, I don't have to take that. You're liable to get backhanded right off that stool someday."

"See if I care one bit. That's all I need. Go ahead if it'll make you happy."

"Forget it. I was kidding."

"Get it out of your system, go on, if it'll do you good, if that's what you need to feel like you're somebody."

"Oh, Christ," said Tully, turning away.

"Knock some teeth out while you're at it. I still got a few of my own in there the others were nice enough to leave me."

"God almighty. I wouldn't hit you."

"It shouldn't be too hard. What you waiting for? There's nothing I can do to stop you. It ought to be a big lift for you. Just the thing you need. Don't let it worry you. Far be it from me to spoil anybody's fun. Go on, since you got your mind made up. If that's how you get your kicks, I guess I'll do as well as anybody else."

Groaning, elbows on the bar, he put his face in his hands and for a moment it was as if his wife were again berating him. "Okay, okay, okay, I'm sorry," he said into his hands, his one impulse to mollify her, to keep her with him by his penitential pose. "I'm trying to tell you I'm sorry, believe me. Listen, I'm sorry. Will you listen to me? I'm *sorry*."

"Well, so what? So you're sorry."

Baffled, Tully was in a turmoil. There was nothing he could do. Caught where he had been so many times before, he felt he would slam his hateful head on the bar if she did not forgive him. "I feel I could just break my head," he said.

"I wouldn't stop you."

"I feel like beating my head on the bar," he warned.

"Go ahead."

With a loud knock his forehead struck the varnished wood. Her hands were on him then; she held him by the shoulder and under the chin and there was strength in her arms. Taking up his glass he toasted the staring faces. He was feeling good again; he had regained his authority.

"What did you want to do that for?"

"You can count on me right down the line," he said.

"You want to knock your brains out?"

"You can count on me. Don't you believe me?"

"I get along all right."

"Listen, let me tell you something. You can count on me right down the line."

"I thought you wanted to hit me."

"Forget that, will you? I never hit a woman in my life. I'm not that kind of lousy bastard. Ask anybody. I won't let a friend down. Let me buy you a drink. Don't you think you can count on me?"

"Just don't bump your head any more."

"Will you forget that? I asked you a question. Do you think I'd let you down?"

"I don't know, would you?"

"I wouldn't."

"Maybe you wouldn't. After all, I mean, how would I know?"

"You can count . . . on . . . me," he declared to emphatic slaps on the bar. "I'm the reliable type. You think I'm kidding, don't you? You can count me among your friends. Don't you believe me? Any time you need anything, come see me. You're all right. I mean that."

"Well, I like that about you. You know who your friends are."

"That's right."

"These others I wouldn't ask for the time of day."

"They wouldn't give it to you."

"You're the only son-of-a-bitch that's worth a shit in this place."

"I appreciate that. I mean because there's something I like about you." Tully sat with his arm around her neck. The crisis was past, the confusing emotions gone so quickly it was as if that brief desperate turbulence had no significance. He felt loose and supple. His scalp was tingling from a sensation of astonishing intimacy. When they went out together he was fondling her curly head. And he was in control now, talking rapidly to allow no interruption, trying to circumvent all possible subjects for contention in order to remain in favor. At the door, during a crescendo of trumpets and guitars, he glanced back over his shoulder in leering triumph, but no one was looking at him. A cooling breeze had risen. The sky was clear; the Big Dipper tilted over Center Street. Tully realized how drunk he was when he stopped on the sidewalk for a kiss and, eyes closed, pleased at finding he was the taller, lost his balance.

Oma had surged against him, and as they walked on, his arm across her back, hers at his waist, she continued to lean against him, forcing him toward walls and store windows.

"You all right?" he asked.

"I don't know."

"Can you make it?"

"I guess I'm drunk."

"I'll get you home. Don't worry about anything. You can count on me. We going the right way?"

When she began to cry, he was moved by a sudden conjugal sympathy. "I love you so much," she said, and it was such an unexpected confession that he felt he had never been so happy. Pulling her up the dark stairway to her room, he felt that from now on everything would be different.

16

Billy Tully's suitcase stood empty in the closet; his coats, slacks and shirts hung from wire hangers, and beside the suitcase and his canvas athletic bag was a carton filled with Earl's clothes that Oma had taken down from hangers and removed from the dresser drawer where Tully's gray underwear now was neatly stacked. The underwear he had ceased wearing, the T-shirts because of the heat, the tattered jockey shorts ostensibly for the same reason, but also abandoned for the sake of virility. He had found that hanging free facilitated desire. He was trying to be compatible. Though able enough, he felt he was a lover more from duty than from inclination. With his wife he had not had to try. From her he had met with reprimands for inopportune fondling, for lingering about, trying to embrace her over the sink or on her way between stove and refrigerator, for entering the bathroom to ask if he could join her in the tub. At times his wife had been coyly elusive, insinuating rewards for deferment, at times cross, shouting that he interfered with her housework and allowed her no peace. Then he had been hurt and sulked on the sofa, silently cursing her and grinding his teeth. Eventually he had gone to her with apologies and contrite embraces that again brought on a burgeoning of desire. That desire, that yearning for her, had been the foundation of his marriage, and after she was gone it had not left him. He yearned for her even while holding Oma Lee Greer in his arms.

On nights when Tully could not bear to hold Oma at all, after hours of bickering had made her so repulsive to him that he shrank from touching her, his desire for his wife was acute. Writhing in the darkness, he pined finally for any woman, other than the one beside him. On other, easier, nights, he enjoyed her with indifferent flamboyant vigor. But afterwards he experienced none of the affectionate gratitude he had felt for Lynn. He lay quietly, oppressed by a sense of dwindling life, of his youth dwindling away as he rested beside a woman he should never have known, here so far off the course he knew should have been his that he wondered with panic if it had been lost forever. He could feel no love, and the anguish of a life without it was greater now than when he had lived alone. Then at least there had been the anticipation; now, though there were comforts, there was no hope except in eventual escape, and of that he did not feel capable. When he imagined escape it was always to his wife that he fled, yet when an argument offered the break with Oma he had wished for, he knew, in the soberness of fear, that his wife was gone from him forever, that the course of his life could be no other than what it was, that without Oma he would be alone, that he was lucky to have her and would have to soothe her, agree with her and try in the future not to vex her. He rendered to her the same apologies and declarations he had rendered to his wife, and afterwards he felt a sad sense of sacrilege. Sometimes after Oma had gone to bed he stayed up with the light out and continued drinking by the open window, through which the warm September air, faint music, voices, the sound of shattering glass, the hum of cars and rumble of trucks entered with flashes of light that played over the sleeping form under the sheet, and he felt the guilt of inaction, of simply waiting while his life went to waste. No one was worth the gift of his life, no one could possibly be worth that. It belonged to him alone, and he did not deserve it either, because he was letting it waste. It was getting away from him and he made no effort to stop it. He did not know how. He fought urges to hurl his tumbler out the window. The chair he sat on smashed in his mind against the wall. Yearning for struggle and release, he felt he had to fight, as he had felt years before when he had come home from the army to begin his life and confronted the fact that there was nothing he wanted to do. But then he had had youth, and several service championships. His mother had died when he was a senior in high school, but his father and a brother and sister had still been in town. Now they were all gone, his father remarried and living in Phoenix, the brother in the Marine Corps, the sister living with her husband at Fort Dix, New Jersey. The last he had seen of any of them was over two years ago when he and Lynn had gone to visit his father prior to kidney surgery. But his father had passed the stones in the hospital and, relieved of the doleful prospect of an operation, had soon begun attacking his summoned offspring with the sarcasm of earlier years. A small red-faced, alcoholic cement finisher with brown teeth and an Oklahoma accent, the old man had got up from the hospital bed, gone home and got drunk. On the back porch, after a shouted quarrel with his father, Tully and his brother and his father's wife had almost fought over the question of how much indulgence a son owed. Since then Tully had written a few postcards, but had seen none of his family. He thought of them with neither fondness nor dislike nor curiosity. He had left them behind, he told himself, the only one still here in the city where they had last lived together.

Tully continued to get up before dawn. Though Oma received monthly compensation for the death of her first husband, he dressed in the dark with the bitterness of one supporting a parasite. While Oma went on sleeping, he ate bread with coffee; if he had time he fried eggs and packed a lunch. Quietly he closed the door and went down the stairs and, as he hurried along lighted streets to the long lines of trucks and buses, a sense of relief at being alone came over him. He rode, sleeping, to peach orchards, where he spent the sweltering days on ladders among leaves filmed with insecticide, a kidney-shaped bucket hanging over his belly from a shoulder harness and thumping his thighs as he ran with it loaded to the train of trailers pulled through the shadows under the trees. By mid-afternoon he was back in the room. In his purple satin robe with BILLY TULLY across the back in white letters, he clopped in unlaced sockless shoes down the hall to the tub.

"You're so handsome," Oma said once as he stood in

the robe after his bath, combing his hair in front of the mirror.

"I am?" Pleased, smiling, he turned, stretched luxuriously, moved to where she sat, and stood over her in coersive silence, a hand at the back of her head urging her to further homage.

In slacks and a short-sleeve shirt, the top buttons open, the sleeves folded up above his biceps, he took her out to eat. On the days when she was not in the room, he found her in the Harbor Inn, and after an early supper in a café crowded with farm workers, they spent the evening drinking.

One night in the sour twilight of Paris de Noche they met Esteban Escobar with a large young woman. Her hair was platinum blond, the pits in her face obscured by a coating of pink make-up, and in her presence Tully felt restricted by Oma; now that he had her he was no longer free to pick up a woman. The four of them drank together, Esteban at times placing an audible kiss on the girl's fat white neck. He wore a well-pressed, tan summer suit, a yellow silk shirt open at the collar and immaculate brown and white wingtip shoes. His flat brown face was immobile, his irises as black as his oiled hair and as inexpressive as a bird's. Tully felt an old ease around him. While never close friends, they had both been at their peaks together, and Esteban had lasted. A Filipino asparagus cutter, he could still draw his countrymen to the arena. He, and the girl beside him, renewed in Tully the belief that his own retirement might only be a protracted layoff between bouts. He asked who was at the gym, talked of past fights, progressed to the subject of mismanagement and eventually to his bout in Panama with Fermin Soto, which he viewed now, for the sake of convenience, as the pivotal event of a long-suspect relationship with Ruben Luna.

"To save a couple hundred bucks he sent me down there alone and blew my chance," he said, and turned to Oma. "You know who Soto was then?"

"Soto. He's the one you fought, isn't he?"

"Oh, for God's sake."

"He was good, huh?"

"Good? I had that bum hanging on. I was all over him like a swarm of flies. I was on that night. I was *on*. You never seen so many sick faces. My own seconds looked sick, those bums. They all figured me for nothing and for six rounds I'm knocking him silly. I had that guy by the ass and there wasn't anybody in that arena didn't know it. So I'm back in the corner, I know I got him, I'm not even paying attention to what they're doing. I don't feel a thing. I just know he's going out of there next round. So I go out and he pops me a couple times and here's the referee stopping it and blood pouring all over me. How do you like that? Both eyes cut. Nobody says a thing. They're all happy. Audience screaming their heads off. Seconds patch me up and put me on the plane, all smiles. Adios. So the first thing I get back to Stockton I go see Ruben and he takes off the butterflies and looks at the cuts and says these were done with a razor." Tully paused.

"Were they?" asked Oma.

"Were they? Sure they were."

"How could he tell?"

"He could tell by looking at them. What do you

think? So we went up to Sacramento to the commissioner and filed a complaint."

"What happened?"

"Nothing." He paused again. The others waited.

"Is that all?"

"That's about the size of it."

They were all silent.

"That was a dirty trick," offered the girl with Esteban.

"That's about it, all right," Tully said, and attempted to generate something more. "I don't know, maybe I should of gone into something else, like insurance. You fight your heart out and what does it ever get you?"

"That was tough luck," said Esteban in a clipped monotone. "Soto's a good man."

"Good? I had that guy beat."

Esteban was leaning again toward his companion. "How about another drink? Tomorrow I take you downtown, get you something nice. You like perfume? I don't care how much it cost, it don't make no difference to me."

"Okay, okay, don't hang on me."

"You like that, baby. Don't tell me you don't like that. I hang on you if I want to hang."

"Aren't you sweet."

"I'm sweet if other people sweet to me."

"I been thinking about giving it one last try," Tully said. "I just let myself go all to pot. I'm going to start doing some running. If I can get in shape I know I can still fight."

"Well, fight then," said Oma.

"I'm going to."

"Sure you are. I've heard that one before."

"I am."

"Sure, sure."

"I mean it, goddamn it."

"Uh-huh."

"Oh, screw you."

"Blow it out your ass, cowboy."

They sat in silence, all facing ahead while an overhead fan with oarlike blades revolved slowly through the heat. Angry, Tully frowned awhile into the mirror so that nobody would think he was stupid enough to be happy with Oma. Soon Esteban's woman began to sigh with obvious impatience and so they all went down the street. Tully pressed against her as they entered a packed bar where a baldheaded man with sideburns and a blond woman with a worn, pretty face were picking electric guitars and singing.

> *Why don't you love me like you used to do?*
> *Why do you treat me like a worn-out shoe?*
> *My hair is still curly and my eyes are still blue,*
> *Why don't you love me like you used to do?*

That night in the room, Tully experienced a desperation he was afraid he could not contain. He felt as if his mind might shatter under the stress of Oma's presence. He could not bring himself to speak, and when she spoke he could not listen. At the sound of her voice he felt he had to get away. Yet because he could not love her, she seemed more defenseless, and he more bound. As assuagement for the loss of his liberty, he longed for a closer attachment. In bed beside her he lay motionless, repelled by the thought of contacting her with even a toe. But her hand sought him. Though he did not yield, it moved with proprietary assurance, until he turned, his foot tangling in the sheet and pulling it from their bodies as he thrust his leg between hers with the savagery of one administering punishment. His exertions made no discernible impression. Afterwards as Oma slept, he was so excruciatingly aware of his structure, of each troubled limb, each restless joint, that he longed to thrash about in search of some position of ease. But he moved slowly, carefully, in order not to disturb her. As he inched up an arm, straightened a leg, his muscles seemed to pulse on their bones in an agony of confinement. He was balked. His life seemed near its end. In four days he would be thirty.

17

In the midst of a phantasmagoria of worn-out, man-
gled faces, scarred cheeks and necks, twisted, pocked,
crushed and bloated noses, missing teeth, brown snags,
empty gums, stubble beards, pitcher lips, flop ears,
sores, scabs, dribbled tobacco juice, stooped shoulders,
split brows, weary, desperate, stupefied eyes under the
lights of Center Street, Tully saw a familiar young man
with a broken nose. His first impulse was to move away
through the crowd to avoid being seen, but they had
both come here for the same reason. He approached
him, calling, and even the name came to him. "Hey,
Ernie." The other looked around blankly. "How's it
going? You making the day hauls now?"

Ernie stood with his hands in his pockets. "Shit, man,
wife's pregnant, I get up in the middle of the night two
times now and come down to pick up a few extra bucks
and run into a mob like this."

"Go out on nuts."

"I won't be going out on anything with all these guys
wanting to get on. You doing this shit?"

"I go out now and then. I don't pick, though," Tully

lied. "I can get on as a checker whenever I want to work. I'll get you on walnuts. How's it going? Been doing some fighting?"

"I fought awhile."

They went down the block to a red bus with a wired-down hood. Framed in the windows were slumped men.

"You go out yesterday?" asked the driver, who was leaning against the fender.

"I was the tree-beater."

Looking at Tully's face for the first time, the driver sucked mucus down from his nose and spat. "Get on."

"I brought you a sacker."

"I'll wait and see if yesterday's crew shows up first."

"You're making a mistake if you pass this guy up. I'll give you my personal voucher, this kid is a nut-sacking fiend."

Looking away, the driver gestured impatiently. "Get on then, both of you."

In the rear of the bus, amid a smell of urine, Tully felt only a moment of importance at getting Ernie a day's work, then his influence began to seem more a matter of shame than pride. Afraid he might appear to be nothing but a farm worker, he began to talk about getting back into shape, finding encouragement in the fact that Ernie, after that disappointing day in the YMCA, had actually become a boxer. Talking while men snored around them, they bounced north past lighted dairies and through powerful odors of manure. The bus stopped on a dirt road among the dark shapes of trees in the gray light of approaching dawn. A tractor was running nearby. Under the trees lay blue-white mist. A truck had preceded them into the grove, and as the men swarmed to it for their sacks and buckets, Tully was called aside by the bus driver, who was standing with the ranch foreman.

"You'll work the tower again. Can your partner hustle?"

"This kid's a great athlete."

"We'll send him with you then. Just watch out for your hands, kid."

The two walked to the idling Caterpillar and Tully climbed up the rungs of the narrow tower hitched behind it—a fifteen-foot metal cylinder, like a drainage pipe mounted on wheels, into which, having reached the top, he lowered himself until his feet were on the platform, his waist level with the mouth of the tube. He pulled up the long pole that leaned against it, held it under one arm like a lance, and the tractor and the tower lurched into motion. Bracing himself with a hip as he rocked and swayed, brushed by leaves, he swung the pole in a sideways sweep. With the first assault, Ernie, under the tree clearing nuts from in front of the Caterpillar's metal track, yelled out in protest, his voice barely audible in the roar of the engine. Tully's second blow sent down another bombardment of green-hulled walnuts. While Ernie shouted up at him, he laughed and flailed again at the tree. Another shower of nuts fell. Ernie covered his head, stooped, rose, throwing, and a nut rang against the tower. The driver motioned him forward. Ernie, his mouth working angrily, ran on to his position in front of the tractor, and Tully, belaboring the branches, saw him gliding in a swift and furious crouch, his hands, deftly knocking aside nuts, darting at times within inches of the advancing track. The crouching figure, the tractor and the tower all turned about the tree as one unit and progressed to the next tree in line. The pole crashed into the branches, Ernie was pelted, and Billy Tully was euphoric. Up near the green treetops in the swaying tube with a view of crawling nut-sackers dispersed over the ground, he wielded his stick with great energy.

The tree-beating ended at noon, and Tully and Ernie joined the others crawling over the clods. Nuts banged into buckets, buckets were emptied into sacks. Covered with dirt, the two talked and scrabbled through the afternoon.

"I'm just a damn fool wasting my time out here," said Tully. "But you get in a bind. I got my responsibilities too. Don't think I don't. I got a woman on my hands and that means getting up at four and breaking your back all day. But if I can start fighting again that'll be the end of that."

"Sure, you'll be making some money anyway. You can sleep in the morning. Anything's better than this."

"It's not just that. I'll flat-ass leave her."

He lifted a full sack and jogged with it to the truck. When his sore knees again dropped onto the dirt beside Ernie, he said: "All I need's a fight and a woman. Then I'm set. I get the fight I'll get the money. I get the money I'll get the woman. There's some women that love you for yourself, but that don't last long. Ernie?"

"Yeah?"

"Take care of that wife of yours."

"I'm trying."

"I envy you. That's the truth, even though you got

to break your back. I was married. I didn't know what a good one I had. Don't let anybody knock marriage, kid. You don't appreciate it till it's gone."

"It's got its compensations."

"That's a fact. That's absolutely right. It's got its compensations. I'd say that's exactly it. You can't get around that. I had it good but I blew it." Rising up on his knees, Tully took out his worn wallet.

"Good-looking," said Ernie, studying the plastic-covered snapshots.

"Redhead."

"She looks stacked."

"She was stacked, all right, and I let something like that get away from me. I tell you, if I had some money I'd send her a plane ticket tomorrow. What I'd like to do is get a couple of fights and rent a nice house. You want to go to the gym sometime? Maybe we could work out again, see how I feel. I was in bad shape last time. I mean don't think I like doing this. You should of seen the house we had. New car. Everything."

And so Tully, relating the story of his marriage, crawled through the afternoon, separating nuts from clods until all nuts were the same hated one thrown forever into the bucket.

18

On the day Billy Tully and Ernie Munger came together through the door of the Lido Gym, a new period
of energy began for Ruben Luna. He had been in a
slump. Only Wes Haynes and Buford Wills were in
training. With his wife and children Ruben felt such
impatience that he rarely could look at them, his eyes
shifting around them as though to lessen his weight of
suffering. On Halloween he had been coerced into
going trick-or-treating, his daughters, in masks and
costumes, running on ahead to ring doorbells while he
came along behind holding the hand of his sheet-
draped son. From the shadows of the sidewalk he had
watched their animation as they filled their paper sacks
with candy, and he felt only the utter dullness of it all,
the meaningless expenditure of himself that he was
powerless to stop, begun imperceptibly long ago in the
name of a love he could no longer feel. The more excited his children had become, the more constricted he
felt, until it was as if his children and his wife, and the
whole town with its porch lights on under a sky of
drifting clouds, were conspiring against his life. To one

neighbor, teasing with hands behind his back, Ruben bellowed from behind a shrub: "Are you going to give those kids that candy or aren't you?" Soon he was not speaking at all. When his children ran across the street without looking, he said nothing.

But with Billy Tully and Ernie Munger back in the gym, Ruben was charged with new purpose. He was imagining a local promotion, headlined by Tully, with Ernie making his professional debut in one of the preliminaries. Now that Ernie was married he would need money. Without it, Ruben was afraid he would again lose interest. It seemed better to risk moving him too soon out of the amateur ranks than to lose him entirely. When Ernie brought his wife to the gym, Ruben, seeing that swollen belly, felt his decision was right.

Rain fell for days. The black surrounding fields, past which Ruben drove his family one Sunday afternoon, were stripped and mired. The rows where choppers, cutters and pickers had stooped through the heat of summer now were only austere lines converging in the distance. Ducks floated on flooded fields among reflected clouds, and through the day their formations were etched high over the city. Down his own street, under bare sycamore trees, his children waded in the gutter. Earthworms, disgorged from saturated lawns, lay drowned on the sidewalk. At night in bed he listened to the wind and the dripping from the eaves. Then there were days of dense fog, impenetrable to the lights of his Pontiac as it crept to the gym.

Billy Tully was sparring now, between rounds leaning over the ropes, panting, his face red, his pulse visible in the pit of his stomach. Crudely painted on his leather cup, worn outside his trunks, was the head of a ram.

"Looking great," said Ruben.

One day he called Owen Mackin, who had promoted at the Civic Auditorium since the days when Ruben had fought there himself. "Owen," he yelled into the phone. "Ruben Luna. Luna. I got Billy Tully back in training. Billy Tully. In training. Owen, I'll tell you what I want for him. A good tune-up fight." He heard Western music from the jukebox in Mackin's bar. "A couple good wins and he'll be ready for the best. But right now I'd like somebody that'll give him a good workout, give him back the old confidence. I don't mean a bum. Maybe some kid ready for main events. What do you think?"

"Tully won't draw."

"He'll draw fine. He's a good clean athlete with a fine record. He's got a lot of class."

"Maybe I could use him in a semi-final."

"A semi? Tully in a semi? He's still got the old stuff. I don't want him in a semi."

"He won't draw."

"We can have a Stockton boy in every bout. I got a fine young welterweight for the opener. I told you about him."

"That's how it stands."

"Munger."

"What?"

"Munger, Munger."

"It's too big a risk."

"Tully's going to be sharp. Come down and take a look at him."

129

"How about Arcadio Lucero?"

"Lucero?"

"I can get him. When's Tully going to be ready?"

"Well, Lucero—maybe five or six weeks—Lucero, I don't know. He's a puncher. What I meant, you know, was a tune-up. Why should I put him in with Lucero when he's just getting in shape? I mean if he had a couple good tune-ups first."

"I think I can get you Lucero," said Owen Mackin.

"Not that I doubt he can take him."

"He made friends here."

"Not that I think he'd ever nail Tully."

"Well, I'll tell you, I think I can get Lucero."

"Wouldn't be a bad win on the record."

"I could phone."

Ruben hung up thinking Lucero used to mean something and knowing he still did in Stockton. Two years ago he had knocked out Manny Chavez a few days before Chavez's picture appeared on the front page with the story of his arrest for selling heroin to a federal narcotics agent. Lucero had returned to fight Mike Cruz, whom Gil Solis had brought out of retirement and then sent back to it with a few hundred dollars and a face already beyond worries of disfigurement even before that final one-round beating. These bouts had won Lucero fans, but Ruben knew the quality of his opposition. What he did not know was whether Billy Tully was any better than the others. Massaging him after his workout, Ruben mused over the firmness of his arms and shoulders. Tully lay face down on the rubbing table in the private dressing room—a windowless cubicle lit by an unshaded bulb and smelling of sweat and liniments, its rough board walls covered with posters of past bouts. Patiently Ruben's fingers kneaded the knotted calves and thighs, wandering, pausing, concentrating at points across the white back, the tanned neck, sinking into damp armpits.

"You asleep? How would you like to fight Arcadio Lucero?"

"Uh. Fight Lucero? What for?"

"I think you can beat him."

"I thought I was going to start out with an easy one."

"Lucero's over the hill. You've still got the stuff. You let yourself get out of shape, that's all."

"Why him?"

"Thought it might be a good fight." His hands grasped, rubbed, squeezed, rose to the taut cords at the base of Tully's neck, finally came to rest and slid away.

"That all?"

"That ought to do it." Ruben, arms tired, spoke in a brisk cheerful voice calculated to rouse Tully to his feet.

"Didn't seem like very much," said Tully, his face still on the table.

"That's plenty. Get your clothes on before you get a chill."

Groaning, Tully struggled to his hands and knees.

That night, after Ruben had gone to bed, Tully phoned. Standing in the dark cold hall, Ruben listened with chagrin.

"All right, I'll fight Lucero if that's the best you can do, and knowing you it probably is. All I want is a fight, and I think you've had your mind made up for you.

But I don't know about you. You never gave a shit about me and I don't give a shit about you and you never will give a shit so why should I? That's what I want to know. If you would of went to Panama—Ruben, I'm talking to you, goddamn it—if you would of demanded those expenses and done that one little thing everything would be different now. Do you know that? I know it, how come you don't know it?"

"Listen now, where are you, what's the problem?"

"What do you mean what's the problem. What's your problem?"

"Now just hold on. Tell me what's wrong."

"You tell me. I'm doing all right."

The conversation trailed off into an exchange between Tully and someone else. He said goodbye, the connection went dead, and Ruben hung up.

"Who was it?"

"Tully. He's been drinking."

Back under the covers, Ruben stared into the darkness, aggrieved that Tully could talk to him like that after all the care and attention he had given him, but aggrieved more at the thought of him drunk. That was a more personal affront, an act of spite. Heavy with foreboding, Ruben was confronted again by the same old frustration of his will, by the inevitable weakness he found in everyone, and for all his efforts could not root out.

The next afternoon Tully was back at the gym.

"You weren't boozing last night, were you?"

"I had a few. Don't worry about it. I was just kidding around."

"You're not going to get in shape if you're boozing."

"All right, I know. You don't have to go through that again."

"Booze is poison to the body."

"I'm off it. I'm not drinking. You got to break loose once in a while. I'm living with a lush—you know how that is."

Through the door of the locker room came sounds of dripping showers and the light bag thumping. "Get rid of her," Ruben said, grave, convinced, uncompromising.

"I know it. I'm going to. I know." Tully's shiny blue slacks dropped down his legs with a clink of change.

19

On the dusty floor of the closet was a clean square where the carton of Earl's clothes had been.

"Is Earl out of the bucket?"

"Huh?"

"Was Earl here?"

"Earl?"

"Did Earl come in here today?" Tully demanded, hanging up his jacket.

"Yeah."

"Why didn't you say so?"

"He was just here long enough to get his stuff."

"Is that any reason for not telling me?"

"I was just going to tell you. You only got in this minute. I didn't have time to open my mouth."

"So how is he?"

"All right, I guess. Didn't have much to say. Picked up his clothes and left. So what's wrong with that?"

With strange anxiety Tully went to the gas plate, tearing open his package of round steak. "You tell him about me? What he say?"

"Nothing."

"He remember me?"

"*I* don't know if he remembered you. What do you care?"

"He remembers you well enough, that's easy to see."

"He had to get his clothes, didn't he?"

"After he found out he couldn't move back in."

"He didn't mention moving in."

"What he come over for then?"

"I told you—his clothes. He knew I was with you."

Tully struck a match and a high blue flame shot up from the burner. "How'd he know that?"

"I saw him before."

"When was this?"

"What're all these questions? He came by the day he got out."

"Why didn't you tell me?"

"I guess I forgot."

"That's a good one." Tully placed the meat in the black encrusted frying pan, pushing in the edge of fat until the steak lay flat.

"What?"

"Nothing."

"I heard what you said."

"Then why'd you ask?"

"You think I'm lying to you."

"I didn't say that."

"You don't trust me, do you?"

"All I'm trying to do," said Tully, now opening a can of peas, "is make us our supper."

"You're so goddamn high and mighty."

"If I didn't cook it we wouldn't eat it."

"Nobody asked you to fix me anything."

"I know. You'd just as soon drink yours."

"If you don't want to make me any, you don't have to."

"I'm making it."

"You'd rather not."

"I got it right here."

"I don't have to eat."

"I'm *making* it for you!" shouted Tully.

"Then I won't eat it if you feel that way about it."

"I *want* you to eat it! I'm cooking it because I want you to eat it. I can't eat all this food myself." Dumping the peas into a discolored pot, he heard her voice again, quieter, sighing, resigned.

"I didn't say anything and you get that pissed off."

He made no reply.

"Now he's mad. He's not speaking."

He turned over the steak in a noisy sputter and stood staring down at the peas until they were violently boiling.

Through the first mouthful of rare meat he said, sitting opposite Oma at the table: "Eat your food before it gets cold." In her hand was a tumbler of wine.

"I don't take orders from you."

"You need your protein."

"I'm not going to eat with somebody who talks to me like you do."

"You want to starve to death?"

"That's what you'd like, isn't it?"

Tully cut off another bloody chunk of steak before saying no.

"That would solve everything for you, wouldn't it?"

"I just asked a simple question," he said, chewing. "Go on, eat."

"Maybe I don't want to eat. Maybe I don't like how it's cooked."

"All right, don't eat it. Go hungry. I don't care. That's good food. I make you a good dinner and you don't even appreciate it. So just forget it. I'll put it away and eat it tomorrow."

As he reached across to her plate, she clutched it, crying: "I want it. I'm going to eat it."

"I don't want you to eat it!" he shouted, pulling on the plate.

"Now you won't even let me have my dinner. You won't even let me eat."

Surrendering, he slumped back into his chair. With tears running down her cheeks, Oma filled her mouth with peas. Tully's appetite was lost under a wave of hostile despair. She's out of her mind, he thought. Feeling suddenly gorged, he forced himself to go on eating, for the nourishment. "So?" he murmured.

"Huh?"

"Well? Do you like it?"

"What?"

"Nothing. Forget it."

"Well, for Christ's sake, don't ask something and then not even say what you mean."

"Supper."

"All right, why couldn't you say it? It's fine."

"I thought maybe you'd know what I meant, seeing as how you're not having any trouble eating it."

"You don't want me to eat it?"

137

"Of course I want you to. I just meant now you're eating."

"I'm eating. Sure, I'm eating."

"So what was the big fuss about?"

Her fork slammed down on the table. "Will you stop needling me? The big fuss is that nobody could eat with you sitting across the table."

"You never had it so good. There isn't another guy in town would make you your supper so you could get something in your gut besides that goddamn juice."

"Very funny."

"I'm serious. Will you show me the common decency of a serious answer?"

"Common decency. You wouldn't know any if you saw it."

"Will you give me a straight answer or won't you?"

"Will you stop doing this to me?"

"Doing what? What the hell are you yelling about? All I asked for was a simple answer."

"You rotten-ass bastard! You're determined not to let me eat this food."

"Oh, for God's sake. I give up," said Tully, pushing back his chair and rising. "All I been trying to do is get you to eat. If you don't want my company just say so and I'll get out of your way." He went to the closet, and as he was taking down his jacket his eyes were drawn again to the dustless square on the floor.

"Where are you going?"

"Think I'll take a walk around the block so you can eat in peace, since that's what you want."

"Can I go with you?"

"I'll be right back."

"You're going out for a drink and leaving me here."

"I'm fighting in a week. You think I'd go out drinking?"

"You won't take me out but you sneak off the first chance you get."

"That's right, everything I do is wrong. Not a goddamn thing suits you, does it?"

"Billy, wait for me. Let me get ready. Just let me comb my hair. Are my shoes over there?"

He went out the door. Her cries pursuing him, he trotted lightly down the stairs. Outside, alone at last, striding rapidly along the wet pavement, Tully experienced a moment of communion with his wife. It was so strong he was sure that wherever she was she must be thinking of him just at that moment. It seemed impossible she would not still be single. Unable to visualize her, he could not imagine her life as anything but emptiness.

In an uptown bar where Oma was not likely to look for him, he felt her presence still depleting him. Now he thought he should have waited for her. Though he did not want her around, he felt guilty for not taking her with him, and he hated her for this inevitable confusion. He seemed unable to do what he wanted. What he did was either what she wanted or else was spoiled for him because it went against her wishes. Tormented, he longed to be rid of her. If Earl wants her he can have her, he thought resentfully. Only why would he? She was white; maybe that was enough. For the first time Tully realized he could leave with a clear conscience. There was someone to take his place. And knowing he had been avoiding that realization, he felt a palpitant anxiety.

Why he phoned Ruben Luna again he was not entirely certain. What he did convey was that he was drunk, because his manager came and got him. "She's destroying me," Tully said in the car. "You're right about this. I know it."

While Ruben's wife, short and plump, in flowered robe and fur slippers, her long black hair in a single braid, stood in the hall doorway, Ruben made him a bed on the pink sofa.

20

The northbound Greyhound droned into Stockton's fume-filled terminal, and among the passengers who filed stiffly out was a short Mexican wearing a camel's-hair overcoat and pointed, high-heeled, yellow gaiter shoes. Arcadio Lucero, with a throbbing head and churning bowels after a long ride from Calexico, pushed open the door to the depot lobby and climbed the steps to the men's room, where, in a dim stall, he stared without comprehension at an inscription scratched across the metal dispenser of toilet seat covers. *Mexican dinner jackets.*

In the waiting room Lucero bought a pack of gum and a newspaper. Chewing vigorously, he carried his bulging, expansible, strap-cinched leather suitcase several blocks to the Lincoln Hotel. In the closet of a room overlooking the lights and traffic of El Dorado Street, he hung the overcoat on a wire hanger. He was dressed in a wrinkled turquoise suit and a white knit shirt. The coat was long, with two low-set buttons. Under it crossed the straps of suspenders and a shoulder holster. With a hand over the long fly of his trousers, his coat open, he lay on the bed listening to the sounds in the street and in his own abdomen.

From Mexico City to the border at Mexicali, Arcadio Lucero had read comic books and slept in a Pullman berth through glaring sun and starlit darkness, past pale barren ground, adobe villages, towns and cities, mountains, desert, then silos and cultivated fields. He had drunk soda pop from tepid bottles carried in buckets through the train, and eaten mostly what was brought aboard or held up to the windows by the crowds of shouting peddlers in a long succession of stops. Barefoot girls and women had come down the aisle with pans of goat meat, great baskets of chicharrones, hot tortillas wrapped in cloths. Boys, men, old toothless women had run along beside the car when the train was again in motion, calling, offering bananas, guavas, mangoes, paper cones of flavored ice, Jello shimmering on the palm of a hand, lifting something up to him and fumbling his money, running faster to give him his change, or slower, grinning, shrugging, as the train pulled away. Somewhere he had bought half a roasted cow's head and eaten it held by the horn with newspaper on his lap. What had caused the diarrhea he did not know. But he had fought with it before, and soon he would go to a drugstore.

Over the voluminous legs of his trousers he opened the newspaper. On a page with a photograph of basketball players, he stared at the columns of print until his name separated itself from inscrutable words. He drew from his pocket a small bone-handled knife, folded the paper along the edges of the article, slit each fold, threw all the remaining paper on the floor, and squinted at the excised article, his lips moving silently at each appearance of his name.

Of Billy Tully he knew nothing and he cared to know nothing. He went where there was work, and who his opponents were no longer made any difference. He worried only about himself, his health, his conditioning, and his hands. Because he had broken his left on the top of a head, he had not fought in four months, and though he had carried the hand several weeks in a cast, it had pained him when he again had tried to hit with it in the gym. So he had rested it, and one day from a peddler outside a church he bought for two pesos a silver milagrito in the shape of a tiny hand. In the church he kissed the painted feet of the Virgin and the hem of her robe, laden with hundreds of silver hearts, legs, arms, horses, cows, pigs, and on a small exposed patch of the purple velvet had pinned his hand. The pain was gone the next time he went to the Baños Jordan and threw his fist against a heavy bag.

He had resumed training and, in debt to his manager, had been quickly matched. On the train he had shadowboxed in the men's room, and at stops along the way had got off and run up and down beside the standing cars. Often in the past he had fought with less training; he had fought without training at all, keeping in shape by fighting sometimes once and twice a week. Since his first bouts as a fourteen-year-old flyweight, he had many times gone into the ring after nights of bedless sleep, with half-healed cuts, broken nose, sore throat, fever, venereal infections, and had learned to have faith in his body. A few times he had been knocked down and had stayed down—not from fear but from the certainty of a severe beating—and that had seemed right too, because his body was his livelihood. Early he had learned how to last, and he had lasted now fifteen years.

Arcadio Lucero had begun with desperate fury and a relentless style evolved in disputes with other shoeshine boys in the zocalo of Oaxaca where, after the death of his mother, he had slept on the benches under the trees. In winter, wrapped in a serape and wearing a knit cap, he had coughed and shivered with other boys and men through nights of semi-sleep, and though he missed his mother he did not miss an earlier comfort. Before her death he had slept huddled with his brother and sister on the sidewalk while she dozed and tended a charcoal brazier with one or two ears of corn keeping warm at the edge of the grate for any late passer-by. A Zapotec Indian, she had squatted through the days at the same spot, selling the corn she seasoned with slices of lime dipped in salt and powdered chili, while he and his brother loitered outside cafés and cantinas and in the dirt streets of the market, driving away dogs, begging, standing watch at parked cars, wagons, loaded mules and burros. Hard blackened ears of corn had been his breakfast until that cold morning when he awoke to a dead fire and saw his mother lying on her side, openmouthed. His sister, the youngest, had died earlier. His brother left town with a farmer, and Arcadio went to the park with a can of wax.

Those first frantic bouts in Oaxaca and Tuxtla Gutiérrez he had fought with grim zeal. Training sometimes in a dirt-floored gym, fighting under rain-drummed roofs with water dripping into the ring, he had moved northward, arriving at sixteen at the border at Juárez, where he stayed long enough to father a child. When he got to Mexico City he was grown, a seasoned and calculating puncher with the scars of a veteran on his broad Indian face. He weighed 126 pounds.

Fighting in the capital, he could afford a suit and new pointed shoes with elevated heels. His thick hair he wore long, combed back over the tops of his ears. Set in one pierced earlobe was a tiny gold medallion. Soon his face was in the tabloids. Then the fans who crowded the floor of the gym closed about him. Young men lined the ropes when he sparred, pressed around him at the speed bag, a boy standing above him on the quaking platform as a steadying ballast against the force of his blows.

The Coliseo was designed like a small bull ring, circular, its tiers of balconies screened off with chicken wire to protect the boxers, referee and ringsiders from thrown bottles and weapons that might have escaped the searching hands of policemen who patted down from armpits to ankles each entering spectator. Often through the chicken wire and up from ringside at the end of his fights, a shower of coins sailed into the ring. Leaving the arena past the lame and blind still moaning and chanting outside the doors, Lucero was followed by a group of admirers. Sometimes as many as twenty, they accompanied him up the unlit street, ingratiating, shouting, waiting with him at each corner for the last of the group to catch up—a smiling young cripple who dragged himself along the pavement on a piece of rubber tire. And there in the dark among glowing fragrant cigarettes, watching the laborious approach of that low twisted figure with helplessly tossing legs, he felt moments of limitless destiny.

He knocked out the national featherweight champion, and after one celebrated year was knocked out himself. He went on traveling, defeating hometown favorites all across Mexico, but the important fights he began to lose. Lucero now was wearing down. He had fought nearly two hundred times. What would become of him after he could not go on he had no idea, so did not think about it. All that was before him was tomorrow's fight, and a week after another in Los Angeles, if he got by this one. A knockout loss would bring a thirty-day suspension.

Out on the street, Lucero found a drugstore with a Mexican clerk. While there he dialed the number given him in Mexico City by his manager, and to the voice that answered said: "Bueno? Gil Solis? Estoy aquí—Arcadio Lucero. Tengo un cuarto en el Hotel Lincoln." With a tinfoil packet of large flat tablets, Lucero went up the street to El Tecolote. In the window was his picture on a poster. He bent over in the dim light and looked at Billy Tully—who was, he saw, not so young either—and at himself. He had gained ten pounds since the photo was taken. Even so, as he entered, it was evident that the bartender recognized him.

"Coca-Cola," he said, mounting the stool. His last night in this city he had spent here drinking. The bar had been full until closing time, the jukebox blaring and strangers embracing him. He remembered being driven in a car crowded with men and women, and remembered firing his pistol out the window into the air.

Lucero put a tablet in his mouth, took a swallow from the bottle and belched through the devious chambers of his nose. He settled into a kind of contentment. The bartender was moving down the bar. From the corner of his eye Lucero saw the faces of his countrymen turning to look at him, and he felt at home, as at home as he ever felt anywhere.

21

After a steak dinner with Ruben and a stroll along El Dorado Street, Billy Tully went back to the Oxford Hotel, where he had been sleeping, sober and alone, for the past week. But in bed early after a day of leisure, he began thinking about Oma and about the fight. Though he had not seen Oma since the night he had left her, he could not grasp a sense of his freedom. He felt that in being here he was doing something wrong, that he was causing her suffering and tomorrow night would pay for it. Scheming his defense, he visualized himself punching and dodging until he became alarmed about insomnia. He turned and sprawled but could not sleep. At what occurred to him as the first light of dawn, he leaped out of bed with a moan of utter defeat and walked into a wall. Peering at his alarm clock, then out the door at the clock over the lighted stairway, Tully comprehended that he had been in bed only an hour. He got back under the covers and perused the Mexican fight results in *Ring* magazine. While finding no mention of Arcadio Lucero, he noted with dismay the number of knockouts suffered in Mexico in a month's time. There had been such a quantity the correspondent had amused himself with an array of synonyms: dumped, demolished, iced, polished off, put to sleep, embalmed, disposed of. And these unknown defeated Mexicans so depressed Tully that he knew, with terrible lucidity, that the sport was for madmen. He turned out the light and dreamed he could not sleep.

Ruben drove him the next night to the Civic Memorial Auditorium, an adobe-colored edifice with fluted columns and statues of openmouthed bears guarding its walkway. Across the lighted façade, below an inscription that began *Tomorrow and Forever* and terminated down at the other end of the building with *Defense of Liberty*, fluttered a blue and white banner: *Boxing Tonight*. A line of early arrivals extended out onto the concrete walk from the general-admission window. In the lobby, filled already with Mexicans and smoke and the shouts of program vendors, a group of local boxers awaited free admission. Past ushers wearing Veterans of Foreign Wars caps, Ruben escorted them to ringside. He went on with Tully to the dressing room, where Ernie Munger, reclining on a table in black shirt and slacks, his raised neck no longer lean but bulging with muscle, greeted them with an absolutely expressionless face.

Ernie fought in the opening bout, watched by Tully from a back seat on the aisle. In the gym Ernie had at times beaten him to the punch and now what he saw was just another preliminary fighter. Ernie's victory, after four rounds, did not ease Tully's mood. He returned to the dressing room and was forcing up nervous belches when Ernie, lips bloody and nose swollen, came in with Ruben and Babe.

"He walked all over that dude," said Ruben, his eyes searching Tully's with concern. "You should be getting ready. How you feel? You feel all right?"

"Fine."

"Dinner set all right?"

Tully could not answer. Openmouthed, he waited.

"Billy?"

There was a small airy sigh.

"Eat something?" Babe whispered.

"Oh, my God, you didn't drink no beer just now, did you?"

A rich rumble rose at last.

"You sick?"

"No."

"He had a good steak dinner. I took him to a good place, but then you can get a bad meal anywhere. You didn't drink no beer out there, did you?"

"Hell no."

"All right, don't get mad. You're down to a fine edge. That's good. Just keep it that way. You're going to take him."

Tully removed his slacks and the new blue shirt and V-neck sweater, socks and underwear Ruben had bought him so he would not have to go back to Oma's room for his clothes. With sweat trickling down his biceps, he pulled on his supporter, pale-blue trunks and shining purple robe. He sat remote and irritable while Ruben, with quick expert turns and folds, wound the cotton gauze into firm bandages from his wrists to his knuckles. The bandages taped, and tested with blows against Ruben's palms, Tully took out his bridgework—his two upper front teeth—and began bobbing and shuffling around the room, shooting out his fists and blowing through his nose.

When Tully came down the aisle, between turning faces, Arcadio Lucero was already in the ring in crimson-trimmed black satin, his Indian profile impassive. Over the back of his robe in winking sequins of vaporous green, blue, red and gold, was an image of the Virgin of Guadalupe. Backed by Gil Solis and Luis Ortega, his seconds for the evening, he waited with an economy of movement, arms at his sides, head lazily rocking. Tully, following Ruben up the steps and ducking through the parted ropes with a jaunty swiftness he had practiced years ago as an amateur, felt only impatience. It was an old charged feeling of having gone at last beyond any deferment. Standing in the ring with a towel over his head, he wanted to fight and be through with it.

The announcement of Lucero's name drew a partisan response from the half-filled gallery.

The robe was tugged off over Tully's gloves, the mouthpiece was fitted around his teeth, and he was alone in the corner, his arms still tan from the fields, his torso pale, a tattooed swallow in flight over each breast.

"Keep away from him," was the last thing he heard before the bell. But Lucero did not come after him. The Mexican waited at the ropes. Tully's first lead drew no response. Wary, he stepped out of range, bounced on his toes, shuffled in, again pushed out his left, and Lucero, taking it on his high-arched nose, swayed back into the ropes. He leaned there, unflinching as Tully feinted, and in a single reflex Tully smashed his jab, cross and hook against that scarred and patient face. Then he was struck by a blow he had not even seen. Grasping for Lucero's arms, he was pounded over the heart. He retreated, bounced, breathed deeply, and as he stepped back in, Lucero catapulted off the ropes toward him, and Tully was stunned. At the end of the round he returned to two grave faces.

Lucero continued fighting on the ropes, sometimes half seated on the middle strand. Yet not until the end of the second round when Tully drove a left deep into the belly and heard him grunt did he realize Lucero's sluggishness might be something other than trickery.

Water streamed down Tully's head. His trunks were stretched open and a cold shock poured over his genitals. Ruben's hands were on his face like a barber's, tilting it, wiping, patting, smearing on fresh Vaseline. The taped bottle rose to Tully's lips and he rinsed his mouth, turned and spat into the bucket.

"I hurt him in the gut."

"Don't trade with him. Move him around."

"He's weak in the gut."

Lucero waited in his corner and Tully closed with him, punching to the body. Held, Tully slapped a right to the kidney and broke away, the thumbs and laces of his gloves passing deftly over Lucero's eyes as he thrust him off. Stepping out of range, he dropped his guard, but Lucero did not pursue. Stalling, Tully bounced and feinted, and standing flatfooted with his arms at his sides while scattered booing sounded in the gallery, he exposed his chin in invitation. Lucero came forward, but as Tully moved farther away, he checked and waited. He would not lead, and so, reluctantly, Tully again moved toward him, dropping his left to hook to the body. In a white concussive blaze he was falling. On his back, struggling to stay upright on horizontal legs, he looked up at the lights and the brown and blue gathered drapery way up at the apex of the ceiling where a giant gold tassel hung, the whole scene shattered by a zigzag diagonal line, like a crack in a window. He did not remember rising, or how he got through the round. All he remembered were the lights, the gold tassel and the shattered drapery, then the eye-smarting shock of ammonia in Lucero's corner, where he had followed him after the bell and where Ruben had come to lead him back to his own stool. The zigzag line cut the ropes. Cold water cascaded over his head. He felt the drag of a cotton swab through a wound over his eye. When he looked up at Ruben's face he could not see his chin. There was a sparkling vagueness to everything, and pains shifted from the top of his head to his temples and the base of his skull. The ammonia passed again under his nose and now he could see Ruben's chin, but it was off to one side of his face.

"How you feel?" The referee, with a jagged line pulsing in his face and his chin out of alignment, was scrutinizing him.

"Okay."

"He's fine," said Ruben. At the bell he thrust Tully up off the stool.

Lucero rushed across the ring, and Tully set himself, covered, was battered and then had hold of the struggling arms. He leaned and held, kept his cut away from Lucero's head, butted him once and was pulled off. He was struck again and once more had Lucero by the arms. The referee tugged and pushed; they were separated. Urged on by the crowd, the Mexican charged, and Tully retreated, ducking, weaving, rolling with punches. Near the end of the round the jagged line was gone from his vision, and Lucero, breathing through the mouth, had slowed. Tully hit him hard in the stomach just before the bell.

In the rounds that followed, Lucero slowed even more, fighting now as if not primarily to win but mainly to last, lashing out when pressed, often not punching at all when Tully jabbed him at long range. Satisfied to gain points with little punishment, Tully hit and moved away. In the tenth round Lucero's pace quickened, but Tully slammed him with a steady report, and after the bell Lucero stood holding the top rope in exhaustion, his face tilted down toward the canvas.

At the announcement that Tully had won, Ruben pulled him to his feet, grasped him around the thighs, and staggering, lifted him up to a reception of moderate applause and scattered but passionate jeering. The towel fell from Tully's head as the two reeled sideways across the ring, Tully's arms rising and falling like wings in an attempt to right his balance. His feet thumped back to the canvas, and Lucero, eyes swollen to slits and nostrils caked with blood, embraced him around the neck. Head to head, grinning through bloody lips, they faced the photographer from the local press, Tully's weary arm held up by the referee and Ruben at his back attempting to drape him with the purple satin robe, his heavy face looming over Tully's shoulder toward the camera.

The ring lights were already off, the crowd no longer seated and the aisles congested when Lucero, again in the black robe with the sequin image, stood with bowed head and raised fists to final meager applause from his disappointed countrymen. He left the ring followed by Tully, and separated by several yards the two plodded with their handlers back to the dressing rooms.

His nose thick and sore, a row of adhesive butterflies closing the wound on his swollen brow, Tully walked out to the lobby, where the night's boxers and their managers had congregated. Arcadio Lucero, now in camel's-hair overcoat and yellow gaiter shoes with cowboy heels, his dark face puffed and solemn, stood with Gil Solis, Ruben, Babe and Owen Mackin. An elderly man with a hearing aid and a large twisted nose, Mackin was patting him on the shoulder, shouting: "You good boy. We like. You good boy." And seeing Tully he shouted: "You put on a good fight, Billy."

"He was great tonight," said Ruben.

"You get it?" Tully asked.

"Everything's fine."

"What's it come to?"

Ruben raised an assuring hand. "It'll be all right, we'll take care of it in a minute." He leaned toward Tully's face. "Looks good. That'll heal up fine, it's nothing." Then he spoke again to Owen Mackin. "Few weeks he'll be set to go again. It'll be a sell-out next time. This guy's great. I defy anyone to say this guy's not great. First fight in two years and he got himself in perfect condition. He don't smoke, did you know that? Never touches tobacco. This fight was just what he needed. He's ready for anybody now. We got a winner here. He's the most colorful lightweight in Northern California. What did you think of my kid in the opener? Wasn't he fantastic? Ernie, come over here."

"Let's go," said Tully.

"We'll go. Just a minute."

Ernie Munger, who had been waiting near the entrance with Faye, ambled over with his hand on her back, her gray jacket unbuttoned and her belly tremendous in a yellow maternity dress. She stopped a few steps from the group, and Ernie came on alone with his hands in his pockets. "I better be going."

"You did great. Wasn't this kid something? First pro fight and he's cool as ice in there. This kid's got heart."

"Guess I better get rolling."

Taking out his wallet, Ruben stepped aside with Ernie.

"Don't give it all to them baby doctors," said Gil Solis, his strained combative face grotesquely smiling, his narrow eyes fierce.

Tully watched Ernie and his wife go out through the open doors. Beyond a dark plot of city lawn and fallow flower beds, a line of headlights was passing through the fog up El Dorado Street.

"I got a good boy there. Home early with the wife. He's got all the moves. He's got class. Ask Tully. He's the guy that discovered him. Am I right?"

"He's okay."

Ruben gave him a pat on the back. "But this boy here—off two years and he's as sharp as he ever was."

"Guess we'll be going," said Gil, his pitted cheeks scored with deep merciless lines, like a bayed ferocious monkey's. "Vámonos, eh?"

Lucero shrugged, shifted his bag, and with an amiable show of white chipped teeth, offered his hand all around.

Outside in the cold, Ruben told Tully he had earned $241. "You been off too long. Next time you'll draw three times that."

"What's my cut come to?"

"Well, I gave you all those advances. I got to collect on some of that, but I don't want you fighting for nothing, either. We got you on your feet now. Three, four weeks you'll be ready to go again. I'll tell you, why don't I just keep paying your room and board?"

"I'm not drinking any more."

"I know, I know."

"I'm not going to blow any of it. That divorce is what messed me up. Now I'm fighting again I want to get back with my wife and I got to have money. Just take your cut and I'll pay my own bills."

Double-parked at the side of the Oxford Hotel, Ruben counted out a hundred dollars. "It's not worth the goddamn trouble," said Tully, and opening the door, looked back at the traffic coming up the one-way street.

"I gave you those advances with the agreement they'd come out of your purse. I got four kids. But once we get another match made I'll stake you. Don't get out on that side, you'll get run over. Shut the door. Get out over on this side." At the same time that Tully stepped out on the traffic side, Ruben left by his own door to make room for him. They confronted each other across the hood. "What did you want to get out on that side for? Why didn't you slide over?"

"What do you care?"

"You can get run into that way."

Tully went around to the sidewalk. "You're just looking out for me every minute, aren't you? Except when it comes time to pay off."

"I never made a dime off you in two years and you been hitting me for plenty. I'm giving you this hundred because you put on a hard fight and you earned it. But that don't mean we're square."

"You think I'm going to catch punches for a hundred bucks?"

"I'll talk to Mackin. Maybe he'll put you on again in two weeks."

"With this cut?"

"It'll heal by then."

"Know why I got this? This is the same place they cut me with that razor blade because you were too tight to go down there to Panama and work my corner."

"That's not old scar tissue. That's a new cut."

"That's what you'd say, all right. Who the hell cares? All I want is the money for my sweat and blood."

"How about a bite to eat? I'll buy you a sandwich. You shouldn't be out in this wind."

"I'm going to bed."

"Come to the gym in a day or two, huh?"

"Yeah, I'll see you."

Tully went in the hotel and up the stairs, but did not enter his room. He only threw in his bag and re-locked the door. Back downstairs in the entrance, he put his head outside to make sure Ruben had driven away before he stepped back onto the sidewalk.

In the Old Peerless Inn Tully had three whiskies with beer chasers, the second pair because the adhesive strips over his cut interested the bartender, who then recognized his face as that on the poster behind the bar. The third he bought to reciprocate and he bought drinks for the man on each side of him. By then the pleasure of celebrity began to diminish and he felt he had become too popular. After several prolonged hand-clasps, he left.

Out in the fog, weary, yet buoyant from the drinks, his mind dulled along with his aches and his energy returning, Tully was free of the sense of impending ordeal that had been with him for weeks. He felt whole, self-sufficient, felt his life had at last opened up and that now nothing stood between him and the future's infinite possibilities. Already he was moving into that unknown and it was good, because it was his own life, untrammeled by any other. Excited by a sense of new beginning, he walked past dark bars, their doors closed against the cold. Few figures were on the sidewalks. Under the low-hanging lights in the poker clubs, vacant chairs separated players around the green-topped tables. Outside the Liberty Theater he stopped to look at the photos of several strippers framed behind glass in silver cardboard stars flecked with dusty glitter, and in a small pad of fat on a slender, pouting girl named Estelle was an exact replica of his wife's horizontal navel. He studied it for some time before going to the box office.

A movie was groaning and flickering as he entered, its narrator proclaiming the virtues of nudism in a grandiloquent baritone charged with reverence for nature. Tully went down the dark aisle to a row near the stage. Slumped on his spine with his head resting on the back of the seat, he looked up at the workings of a great blurred rump. It was an old film, marred by dark shadows and dancing specks of light, and was spoiled for Tully by implacably positioned tropical foliage. Soon his eyes were closing in the drone of that voice.

". . . and Rama vowed never to return to the world of dresses and tight shoes and all the restraints her upbringing had heaped upon her head. This was her domain, to live in as woman was intended to live, on a diet of sunshine and fresh air, caressed by the cool stream where—what was this?—there were fish for the angler who was quick enough to catch one with her bare hands!"

Tully sat up, squinting. Slouched about the small theater were other isolated men, squinting, yawning, some asleep under the sudden glare of the houselights. Tully waited in line at the lavatory, and when he came back to his seat the theater darkened and the maroon curtain jerkily parted. To the amplified music of a phonograph, the women came out one by one in velour and satin and sequined net, in floor-length gowns with grimy hems and long black gloves split at the seams. Middle-aged, they two-stepped across the stage, pulling off the gloves, pausing at the proscenium to expose a mottled thigh and shake a finger at the audience for peeking. The gloves were tossed to the wings, the gowns dispatched, fringes rose and fell, waved and jiggled. Unclasped brassières were held in place while orange and platinum heads shook in coy demurring. Released, breasts descended, blue-white, bulbous, low, capped with sequined discs. Fringed girdles off, haunches flexed and sagged, satin triangles drove and recoiled. Calves sinewy, thighs dimpled, scars tucked in the fat of bellies, the women rocked and heaved, beckoned with tongues, crouched and rose with the edge of the curtain between their legs. Mouths open, they trotted out on the runway in high heels, squatted, shook, lay on the floor, lifted legs, caressed themselves, rose and ran off with little coy steps, wriggling dusty buttocks. Estelle appeared last, revealing meager breasts, sharp hipbones, and a belly that had lost its plumpness since the pictures outside were taken. There was nothing about it to remind Tully of his wife. Where there had once been such a voluptuous declivity there was now only an unexceptional navel. He left with the same dissatisfaction he had felt every other time he had been here since the days before his marriage when he had attended with Ortega and Chavez. Only then they had driven out of town afterwards, in his Buick or Chavez's Cadillac, and gone to a whorehouse at some small valley or mountain town or at a junction on the road to Yosemite. Once they had driven as far as Nevada. Now Chavez was in prison and Ortega had gone home to his family after sticking his head in the dressing room to congratulate Tully on his victory.

He felt remote, distracted, felt that after having beaten Lucero he deserved a woman. A weary, intangible confusion hovered in his mind, a sensation of forgetfulness though there was nothing to remember. He was walking not in the direction of his hotel but toward Oma's, feeling capable of knocking on her door, of saying he had come only for his clothes, of putting them in his suitcase and then methodically stripping her, taking her without the slightest intrusion on his isolate self, then picking up his suitcase and leaving forever.

Her light was on, showing under the door. He knocked, and even when Earl opened the door, Tully's equilibrium was not disturbed. The dark eyes, the whites a smoky gray flecked with brown, looked down into his with suspicious recognition.

"What you wants?"

Nor did this affect Tully's mood. "Come for my clothes."

"I'm living here," said Earl, as if a misunderstanding persisted. "I pays the rent."

Tully nodded.

"Got your things in your suitcase all ready to go." Earl stepped back and Tully saw Oma on the bed. Leaning against the headboard, she wore a pink dress that exposed her collarbones, the skirt fanning out on the green chenille spread, her legs in nylons, one foot shoeless, the other in a white pump. A tan sweater lay over her shoulders, and as he entered she drew it around her elbows.

"Oh, Jesus Christ," she said.

Tully, conscious of Earl watching him, tried not to appear too familiar. "How you doing?"

"Oh, Christ, Mary and Joseph, look who's here."

"Your suitcase right over there in the closet," murmured Earl. "I'm wearing one of your T-shirts. I take it off for you."

"Don't bother. I got plenty."

"Will you look what the cat dragged in."

"I got my own. Just wasn't none clean today." Earl was already unbuttoning his gray and white striped shirt. He threw it on the bed, pulled the T-shirt, tight, short, yellowed under the sleeves, over his head, uncovering a dark muscular trunk. "What's yours is yours. Oma want me to throw your stuff out, but I say a man's stuff is his stuff, when he show up around here I want to send him off with what he come for." By now the T-shirt was in Tully's hand and Earl was rebuttoning the striped shirt on his way to the closet. Tucking in the tails with one hand, he brought Tully his suitcase.

"You can take that and shove it up your ass," said Oma.

"You hush now. He just come for his things and he leaving."

"Don't hush me, you bunch of bums. What do you know about it, anyway?"

"Don't pay no attention to her. She been drinking."

"Get that shitbird out of here."

"We been out on the town tonight."

"Take the shirt off a man's back. If that isn't just so perfect. If that isn't just like him."

Earl edged toward the door. "She just like to blow off steam. Don't listen to her. We gets along. How I handles her, I just don't pay her no mind. Thing you got to understand about her is she a juice head."

"I know," said Tully. "And she won't eat, either."

"It all on account of her unhappy life and all that

shit, and there nothing I can do about that, so I don't let it worry me. Look like you had your fight. How you come out?"

"I won."

"That right? I seen you on the poster. Like to watch a good fight now and then. Maybe I catch you some time. But they no point in you coming around here no more. She don't want to see you. Oma, you wants to see this man?"

Oma, her brown curly hair in disarray and the broken bridge of her nose shining under the overhead light, replied with an incoherent oath and kicked out her foot, her shoe flying off toward them and falling on the floor.

"You see how it is. I been away—man give me some shit and I don't take shit—now I'm back. You a fighter, you know what I'm talking about. They a right way and a wrong way to take care of yourself."

"That's right," agreed Tully.

"One thing I don't need is trouble. Man see trouble coming he better off walking down the other side of the street. You got your stuff."

Tully raised his hand, still holding the T-shirt, to Oma. She did not look at him. Earl closed the door.

To hell with her, Tully thought, going down the stairs. Don't think you're hurting my feelings. To hell with you, lousy bitch. That poor sucker can have you.

Before he had reached his hotel a ghastly depression came over him, a buzzing wave of confusion and despair, and he knew absolutely that he was lost.

22

Tully was drunk for several days before he changed hotels, and the strange thing about that melancholy time was that he did not think of his wife. It was as if in losing Oma he had lost his love for Lynn. It had been overwhelmed by the monumental misery of the present. He yearned for Oma. Desolate, he could think of no relief but her. When he rememberd how she had irritated him beyond endurance, he detested himself for his weakness; if he had loved her before as he did now, he could have tolerated her. But his love had come too late. That he had not felt it before was reason for bewilderment. For his wife he felt nothing. She seemed not even to exist.

Ruben came on the third day and found him in bed. Outside it was already dark. The rain that had kept Tully in the room with a fifth of whiskey and a loaf of whole-wheat bread was still falling. At first he had not responded to the knocking, but after a moment of keeping silent, afraid it was Ruben out there in the hall, he began to think it might possibly be Oma. When the knocking came again he called: "Who is it?" And he heard that composed inevitable voice.

"Ruben."

There was nothing for Tully to do but open the door. After he did so he got back under the covers. Ruben switched on the light and stood at the foot of the bed, his hands around its scratched metal tubing.

"Billy, you can talk to me. What is it? Why you doing this? Is this any way to treat your body?"

"I don't know."

"What do you mean you don't know?"

"I didn't do nothing."

"You're going to ruin yourself with that stuff."

"Only had a few shots."

"Why didn't you come to the gym yesterday? Work up a little sweat be good for you. Let me have a look at that eye."

"Been laid up with a cold."

"I was by yesterday and you weren't in."

"Must of been asleep."

Ruben was now removing the adhesive strips from Tully's brow. "I looked through the keyhole. You weren't here."

"Out to eat, I guess."

"Looks good. Think I can leave these off. You're still a good healer. Be a nice firm scar. You could go again in two or three weeks. You won, so what you boozing for? You stink, I mean it's disgusting. You're not fooling anybody. I can see what's going on."

"You don't know how bad I feel."

"Pains?"

"I'm hurting, all right."

"Is it your kidneys?"

"Lost my girl."

166

"That all that's wrong? You sure? What girl's that?"

"My *girl*. Left me for a colored guy and I just sat around and let it happen and now I'm sick over it. Should of cut him from asshole to belly button."

"That same one? You left her."

"It wasn't my idea. You're the one made me move out."

"I didn't have a thing to do with it. You wanted to leave her. So I gave you the room rent. You don't want a pig like that tied onto you, fine young athlete with your future still ahead of you."

"I just needed a few days to myself, then I was going back to her."

"You said you were going back to your wife."

"How could I go back to my wife? I don't even know where she is. And I don't want to know."

"You don't want that other one, either. She can't give you nothing. You can get a thing like that on any street corner."

"Don't call her a thing. I'll get up and belt you one. There's nobody like her on any street corner. There's only one her."

"If you'd get up and come down to the gym you'd work this out of your system. Anybody'd think about women, laying in bed all day."

"I'm just sick over it. I can't think straight. Think I want to fart around the gym after something like this? I never felt so bad in my life."

"You're a lot better off without her. You can take it from a man with a family. I'm settled. My mind's at ease. You guys run around making love in bars don't know what a good woman is."

"I'm just sick about it, the way I bungled this thing."

"Let's go out and get you something to eat."

"Not hungry."

"Come on."

Tully slid farther under the twisted blankets. "What do you care? I should never listen to you anyway. You're the one got me into this and now you don't give a shit."

"Well, I'm sorry about it, but everything'll work out for the best."

"You don't give a shit about what I'm suffering."

"Tough, I know. Why don't I come back tomorrow? I'll pick you up and take you to the gym. So keep yourself clean. I want you in shape for a workout."

"You don't know," Tully mumbled, and as Ruben went on talking, he pretended to drowse.

The next day Tully lurched down the stairway with his bags. Leaving no message for Ruben, he moved to the Owl Hotel. After resting on the sagging bed, one foot on the floor to slacken a sensation of backward sinking, he went down to the street to approach nourishment obliquely, drinking a Bromo Seltzer at the Old Peerless Inn, then eating a pig's knuckle. Hours later he returned to the Oxford Hotel and found his key no longer worked.

On the days and nights that followed and became indistinguishable in his memory, he pined for Oma and abhorred his unfathomable stupidity. The thought of existing alone produced instants of vertigo. On waking after a night of arrested falls, hammering heartbeats and sudden breathless staring, he quailed before the emptiness of the day ahead. Without Oma he felt incapable of anything. He could not bear the thought of training, not only because of the effort he could never summon from himself now, but also because the idea of fighting was disorienting in its repugnance. He felt that everyone at the Lido Gym was insane.

One night he awoke sitting up in bed with the dusty curtains, still on their rod, ripped down and covering his head. In his dream he had been accompanying a beautiful woman through a train in search of privacy, until she had disappeared into some compartment and he had run through the car trying doors, meeting only a featureless man, whom he had begun to strike. It was all forgotten in a moment of thrashing panic under the curtains. When he hurled the rod to the floor, a mumbling voice swore beyond the wall.

In the morning waking was like a struggle with death. Exhausted in the dismal sheets, hearing the coughing, the hawking and spitting in other rooms, he sank and rose between consciousness and sleep for nearly an hour before dragging himself up and crossing the cold linoleum to urinate in his washbasin. He was laden with remorse. His life, he felt, had turned against him. He was convinced every day of it had been mis-lived. His attention dulled, his ears humming, a sense of emptiness and panic hovering about him, he feared he was losing his mind. Catastrophes seemed to whisper just beyond hearing.

After dark he walked by Oma's hotel and stood below her window until a police car slowly passed. But the following night when he entered the Harbor Inn and saw her with Earl, his first impulse was to turn and go out. His pride took him to the bar, where with studied casualness he had the quick drink of a busy man. He was sure they had seen him. Whenever he glanced at them they were looking away; and he was surprised that Oma did not attract him. He felt nothing, no vengefulness, no familiarity, no desire. He was not even interested. He went out with a sense of relief and was a block away before feeling the impact of the encounter and the shame of his inaction. Later, in bed, he evoked her for a few sad moments with his lips against the sheet.

His jaws bristled with rust-brown stubble. A gray coating covered his tongue like mold. Intending to wash his socks, he postponed washing his feet. And his thoughts all flowed back to regrets. Sometimes, encouraged by signs of tolerance, he bought a drink for someone on a stool beside him; but these companions seemed invariably to lose interest in his unhappiness and he felt his generosity was accepted under false pretenses. One man, in loose pinstripe trousers and Eisenhower jacket, he slammed against a jukebox and chased outside and up the street for an entire block, the pursuit continuing into the next block at a walk, the man glancing back over his shoulder while Tully shouted.

Bemused, he sat in theaters resounding with hoofbeats and gunfire. He paid his rent by the day, then not at all, meeting the bundled and palsied, gray-faced clerk with hearty promises, until one evening there was a different padlock on his door. Downstairs he argued, shouted, hit the counter, and not having the money to redeem them, he left without his bags.

He went to the Azores Hotel, down near the channel, and an old man with broken capillaries puffed up the stairs ahead of him to unlock a cold narrow room. Over the rippled wallpaper on the ceiling were large stains the color of tobacco juice.

When Tully came downstairs into the bleak, stinking bar, lit by unshaded bulbs hanging from long cords above a row of derelicts hunched over glasses, the bartender was roaring at a woman. Her stool stood in a puddle. Waistless, fat-necked, her face and ankles swollen, her bruised legs spotted with scabs, she sat holding her drink in her lap, out of the bartender's reach, and declared indignantly that she was not going to leave until she finished it.

At noon the next day Tully ate a bowl of oatmeal covered with sugar. He drank coffee sweet as syrup and went on to the Harbor Inn for a glass of wine. Later he bought a fifth and set off to find a warm place to drink it. A cold wind was scuttling papers along the gutters. Dark clouds lay over the delta fields visible to the west beyond the tanks of the gas works that rose from green nettles and fennel and wild oats on the bank of Mormon Slough. In the reeking entrances of vacant storefronts, men in overcoats, sitting on flattened cartons, looked out with rheumy eyes.

Locked in a stall of the men's room of the public library, Tully sat with his bottle in the same morose stupor that had delivered him from so many days, yearning for Oma, who already had begun to fade from his memory and become fixed and disembodied and eternal in his being. He left after prolonged pounding and finally the intrusion of a custodial face under the stall door.

Out on the street under a turbulent dusk sky, he encountered a flow of pedestrians hurrying from closing stores. Unheeded in their midst, a shouting Filipino evangelist gesticulated with a trumpet. Frail, elderly, and suffering with loose dentures, he stood before a music stand on which, fastened with clothespins, sheets of paper fluttered. Tully, swaying in a wide stance, paused on the corner, and the small man, pacing the street near the curb, zealously harangued him. Understanding nothing but a few recurrent phrases in the torrent of jargon, Tully felt he was being taken for a fool.

"Piss on you," he said, moving a few steps away to the crosswalk, where, from the curb, he addressed each oncoming pedestrian: "Piss on you and piss on you," until the evangelist began playing *Tea for Two* on his trumpet.

Tully was a block away and still hearing those halting notes when it began to rain. His hair and the shoulders of his jacket were soaked before he reached shelter in the nearest bar. There he remained, listening to the splash and beat of the rain, aware of cold windy openings of the door as men entered with upturned collars or went out, feet pounding on the wet pavement. To the conversations on either side or to the room in general he contributed a few remarks: "Just because they're sitting on that little hair mattress they think they got life by the balls . . . I served my country . . . You ought to be ashamed of yourselves . . . What's your name? . . . Better watch yourself . . ." On rising sea rolls of nausea, his mind lapsed, his head sank to the bar and he drifted in a vast circle. He remained there until impelled to the lavatory; then he tilted slowly over with his stool, crashing painlessly and without sound to the floor. He became aware of hands under his arms as he tried to rise. Upright, gripped around the chest from behind, he was propelled out the door, his protesting voice sounding far away, as if from another room: "Let me alone, I'm all right."

He revived standing on the sidewalk holding on to a windowsill. He tried to tuck in his shirttails, forgot them, took a resolute step and in a forward plunge was running, striving to stay up, afraid of the damage of falling, then not caring. He struck the pavement face-down and lay for a moment feeling an odd pride that it had not hurt. When he rose he discovered blood running from his nose. Sitting in a windy doorway, he stanched the flow with his handkerchief. Cars splashed by, figures ran past, neon flickered in the rain. Tully rose and with a hand on walls and windows he progressed down the sidewalk to the corner, where he stood awhile before venturing diagonally across the street amid sounding horns and on to the Azores Hotel. He was stopped at the office at the head of the stairs by the red-faced clerk.

"Want something?"

"Just going to my room."

"You don't have no room here."

"I was here last night."

"So where's the rent for tonight?"

"Pay you in the morning."

The clerk motioned toward the stairs.

"Just want to go to my room."

173

"Get out of here."

"Don't tell *me* to get out, you son-of-a-bitch. You talking to *me* like that?"

"Go on, get moving."

"Don't you tell *me* to get moving. You don't tell me nothing."

Tully went back down the stairs and into the rain. Midway in the next block, in the dark recessed entrance of a store, he stumbled against something and was kicked. Cursing, he backed away and sat down on the concrete.

"I'll cut your throat," said the man farther inside. "I got your number. I'm wise to you. Keep your hands off me. You come back here again I'll stick you."

"I'll come back and kick the shit out of you, you don't shut up."

"I'm ready for you."

Rain was blowing in on Tully, and after judging that he had remained long enough to show the other that he was not intimidated, he got up and tried the doors of several parked cars.

On a dark quiet street, in an asphalted loading area strewn with refuse, Tully came upon a great steel incinerator. Cylindrical, the chamber rose well above his head, funneling up to a flue. He had noticed its thick silhouette against the wall of the supermarket, and now in the beat of the rain he felt around its rusty surface and found the door. He swung it open, leaned in and his hand contacted cardboard cartons.

"Who's in there?" He climbed in. Under a soft ringing he felt around, clearing a place for himself among crates and boxes and finding a quantity of shredded

174

paper. This he threw to the center, where the chamber's breadth permitted him to lie full length, and he settled into it with a groan of relief. But he was in a draft. He crawled to the square of dim light, thrust his arm out into the rain and pulled the door almost shut. The chamber now was completely dark. He lay back and burrowed into the paper. Once he thought he heard a truck grinding by, but then he was riding it himself, going somewhere down a long straight road.

He was sick, overcome by repugnance and despair. Aware of nudgings against his foot, he opened his eyes to muted daylight and had no understanding of where he was. Facing him in a rectangle of light was the upper half of a young Chinese in a green smock.

"Come on. Out. I got trash to burn."

"Who the hell are you?"

"Come on. What you think this is, a motel or something? Get out."

"Don't tell me what to do."

"Come on, come on. You crazy? You're going to get killed some day, you don't watch it. Get out. What's the matter with you? You don't even want to move when somebody's going to light a fire under you? You going to lay there and argue?"

Tully rose, his feet sinking, and he climbed out the door. Squinting irritably, he cleared his throat, spat, leaned forward and with the aid of a finger blew one nostril and then the other. Crinkled strips of white paper clung to his clothes. The rain had stopped. It was early morning, cold and cloudy. The young man in the grocer's smock began throwing cartons into the incinerator.

That afternoon Tully arrived at the gym. There were bloodstains on his jacket; he was dirty and unshaven, and it was all the fault of a lousy hotel clerk, he said, an explanation that did not lessen the anger in Ruben's eyes.

"Where the hell have you been?"

"I got locked out of my room."

"Why haven't you been down here?"

"I would have been. I'm ready to start training but I don't have my stuff. I don't have the money to get my bags out of hock. What can I do?"

Ruben gave him a dollar and told him to wait, and after Tully had eaten hamburgers and drunk a milk shake standing in the gym, and after he had showered and waited until the last boxer had gone back to the locker room, Ruben drove him to the Owl Hotel and redeemed his bags.

"I'll be at the gym training tomorrow," Tully promised out on the sidewalk, and Ruben gave him fifteen dollars.

Tully went to bed early that night, full of chicken-fried steak and mashed potatoes, and hearing the sounds of the street, he drifted in the darkness with his loss.

23

The rains ceased; new green leaves covered the elms and sycamores lining residential streets. When a haze of peat dust again hung over the town, Luis Ortega told Ruben that he had talked with Tully. Ruben had not seen Tully since he had given him those fifteen dollars, an error he still regretted. Tully had said he was working as a cook, Ortega reported, but his face was dirty and there was a straw hat on the bar. He had talked about getting into shape.

As summer approached, hundreds of men were again on El Dorado Street, leaning against storefronts, cars and parking meters; and Ruben, passing from his house to the port and from the port to the gym, looked among them for Billy Tully. He did not expect to see him. When Tully wanted to fight again, Ruben believed he would come back to the gym. Until he did, he could only wait. But he did not hope. He had given up on him once already and been disappointed by too many others. As if in rebellion against his influence, they had succumbed to whatever in them was weakest, and often it was nothing he could even define.

They lost when they should have won and they drifted away. Over the years he would see one around town. A few he read about in the newspaper—some fighting in other towns for other managers, one killed on a motorcycle, one murdered in New Orleans. They were all so vulnerable, their duration so desperately brief, that all he could do was go on from one to another in quest of that youth who had all that the others lacked. There was always someone who wanted to fight. He had Ernie Munger, Buford Wills and Wes Haynes; Luis Ortega was back in training, and so Ruben went on.

Ortega had once been a middleweight. With his shoulders hunched around his ears, his chin on his chest, he had stalked, flatfooted and perpetual, through round after round of punishment and won a string of main events by knockouts. Between bouts he had gone to fat. Unequal finally to the added effort and deprivations of conditioning, he had retired. When he returned to the gym, encouraged—Ruben knew—by Tully's victory over Lucero, Ortega was fifty pounds overweight.

Ortega's face was bloated. His sharp-bridged nose curved sideways, his arched brows were split, and he kept an impeccable mustache. On the backs of his plump hands were old homemade tattoos, faded pachuco crosses. His belly and buttocks wrapped in sheets of plastic under a bleach-spotted sweat suit, a pair of tight trunks over the pants and a terry-cloth bathrobe over everything, his great chin jiggling, he produced an abundance of grunts and sweat, but it was clear to Ruben that Ortega would never be a middleweight again. At last he matched him with a young heavyweight in Salt Lake City, securing a preliminary bout for Ernie Munger, who was back in the gym after an absence of several months. Five days before the fight, Ortega, weakened by steam baths, came down with flu. Ruben phoned for a postponement, but Ortega was replaced by a substitute. Now there were no longer travel expenses for three; there was only bus fare for Ernie.

"I'll have to send you up alone," Ruben said. "You can take your guy easy. You'll have a nice trip, knock him out and come back with a few bucks for the wife and kid."

"Go by myself?" asked Ernie.

"It's the expenses. How can I go? There's no expenses for me any more. You want a fight, don't you?"

"I want a fight."

"I mean between you and me I begin to wonder about some of these guys. Who can you count on any more? If it wasn't for you kids I guess I'd just quit."

24

Ernie arrived in Salt Lake City on the morning of the fight and strolled yawning in the shade and sunlight along broad, tree-lined streets where water flowed in the gutters. He stared up at the granite spires of the Mormon Temple and ate ham and eggs while reading the sports page. So the fans would know he was white, Ruben had listed him as Irish Ernie Munger, over Ernie's protest that there was no Irish in his family.

Listless after a vibrating night of open-mouth sleeping on the Greyhound, Ernie bought a magazine and took a room in a lobbyless hotel, where he rested most of the day. His was the opening preliminary, and he believed afterwards that if he had not felt so torpid and had warmed up thoroughly he would not have been knocked down by the first punch of the fight. It caught him cold—a right to the jaw thrown by an opponent with a ruddy rural face and a body as rangy as his own. Ernie dropped to his hands and knees, sprang up before a count and was slugging back without fully realizing what had happened when the referee intervened to wipe the resin dust from his gloves. Then, stunned by blows as powerful as the first, his knees sagging but resisting, he was not even aware of being hit, only of impact already past and survived; and he knew he would not go down again, that the straining face he was smashing could not summon the power to overcome him. Punching with deadly excitement, he sensed he was going to win, saw it in the other's altered stance and in his eyes, and he rushed forward, belaboring the suddenly blood-smeared face until his opponent lay out of his reach.

Elated in the dressing room, he wanted to return to Faye, and to his infant son, for whom, until this moment, he had not yet been able to feel any love. Now he believed it was for them that he had come all this way and fought. On the ride up he had decided he would hitchhike home and save half his expense money, and now he wanted to set off. He was elated by the shower over his body, by the feel of the towel, by simply being himself here pulling on his clothes, hearing the muffled shouts of the crowd.

Conscious of recognizing glances, he came back into the arena. The main event ended with Luis Ortega's substitute, an overweight Negro, sitting on the canvas. The spectators filed up the aisles, Ernie, full of hot dogs, was paid his fifty dollars, and ten of it he gave to the two nervous men who had seconded him. A half hour later he was on the highway at the city's edge, standing near a closed service station, his thumb directed west.

A silent man took him to the airport turnoff. There, with his canvas bag at his feet, the lights of the airport in the distance behind him, Ernie waited on the gravel shoulder, blinded by the swift approach of headlights and left behind with fluttering pants cuffs. From one car something came flying in a chorus of derisive howling, striking the ground near his feet. In the lights of the following car he saw a paper milkshake cup rolling along the shoulder, and spots on the legs of his pants. A plane roared out over the desert, lights winking green and red in the black sky.

In time a car swerved off onto the shoulder beyond him, dust streaming up over the glowing taillights. Ernie ran toward it, and ran on and on, the car braking, then coasting, as if the driver had changed his mind and was starting off again. But the brake lights once more glowed bright and the car came to a stop. When Ernie jogged up beside it the door swung open and he saw two young women peering out at him.

"Hi. Sit up here," said the one by the open door. "The back's full of junk."

Flustered, he ducked in, dropped his bag in back and slammed the door. The light went out, the car lurched ahead, the tires roared on the gravel, and Ernie, who before his marriage had spent so many futile nights looking for pickups, sat in wonderment at women like these.

"Where you going?" asked the one beside him.

"California."

"Yeah? So are we," she said, and he was thinking of motel accommodations when the driver asked: "What town?"

"Stockton."

"What would anybody want to go to Stockton for?"

"That's where I live."

"I guess it takes all kinds to make a world," said the driver.

"Where you going?"

"Where we're going is a matter of conjecture, but we'll get you down the road a way." The driver was tall and, Ernie could see in the approaching lights, powerfully constructed. Her dark hair, combed back at the sides, was cut like a man's. Her chin was heavy; she wore glasses, jeans, and filled a plaid shirt with a large bosom. Her companion was smaller, with blond hair cut in the same style, her face plump and slightly haggard, her hips, in jeans, wide on the seat.

The car hummed on and now the road ran along the edge of Great Salt Lake, the water vast, motionless and black, with a stripe of lambent moonlight extending toward the car. Bathhouses, piers, a dark pavilion loomed on its shore, passed and fell behind. Along the sides of the road the sand glowed white in the beams of the headlights. On the left a range of mountains stood darkly against the sky.

"How long were you out there?" the woman beside him asked after a prolonged silence.

"Quite a while."

"Nobody'll give you a ride up here. They're all Mormons. I saw you were just a boy so we stopped. We've seen other guys along the road, but we didn't pick any up."

"Hard cases," the driver interjected.

"They're probably all still standing back there. I don't know what finally happens to them."

"Somebody picks them up and gets rolled," said the driver. "Tough guys. You can have them."

"Not me."

"You can have them, baby."

"I don't want them."

"You want to help out, they're all yours."

Ernie listened to this exchange with misgivings and decided he would not mention his bout. When asked what he was doing in Utah he answered: "Business venture."

"Business?" said the woman whose thigh rocked at times against his. "At your age?"

"I'm not so young. I got a wife and a baby."

"You don't either."

"I do too."

"Do you really? You look so young."

"You don't have to be old to have babies," said the driver.

"Well, it's good to have babies," contested the other. "What's wrong with having babies?"

"I didn't say anything was wrong with it."

"You implied it."

"I did not. If he wants to have kids that's fine with me. Why should I care?"

"Well, it didn't sound like that when you said it."

"I can't help the way I sound."

"Never mind."

They passed through a settlement and Ernie studied the profiled face beside him, believing that preferences had been established, though what was expected of him now he was not sure. Surrounded again by desert, they raced on. Far ahead points of light appeared and drew closer, shifted down to the road or remained in high cones, glaring in the eyes of the three squinting out the windshield, the dimmer clicking on the floor, the woman behind the wheel saying: "Son-of-a-bitch." After a considerable time of alternated silence and pointless talk, Ernie let his leg fall lax against the plumper leg beside it. The woman did not move. The two thighs jiggled together through miles of humming darkness.

"You going to be able to drive, Noreen?"

"I can drive."

"Because when I give out I'm going to give out all at once."

"Want me to drive now?"

"I'm holding up. Don't worry about me."

"Any time you want me to drive just say so," Noreen murmured, her eyes closed.

"Just stay awake, that's all."

"If we get sleepy we can pull over for a while," said Noreen.

Ernie moved his head closer to hers. A few vagrant hairs tickling his face, he asked, almost whispering: "Do you camp out by the road?"

"We've been camping two weeks in Yellowstone."

"Weren't you afraid of bears?"

"Bears you don't have to worry about."

Wondering if everything had somehow been already decided, Ernie turned his face toward her and waited. She gave him no sign. Finally his eyes closed, and he felt the plastic ribbing of the seat cover sliding slowly under his cheek until his nose came into contact with a soft neck smelling faintly of unwashed skin—like clean, scorched laundry—and of tobacco. He nuzzled it automatically and there was no response, not the slightest movement or tension. She appeared to be asleep, but then she was speaking beside his ear.

"Gail?"

"Huh?"

"You all right?"

"Yeah."

"Don't fall asleep at the wheel."

"I won't."

"Do you feel like you might? Do you want me to talk to you to keep you awake? I don't want you to get in a wreck. That's all we need. So what are you thinking about?"

"Nothing."

"So let's talk."

"There's nothing to talk about."

"You don't want to run us into a tree, do you?"

"There aren't any trees."

"Aren't there? That's right. When are there going to be some?"

"Not for a long time."

"Are we still out here?"

"What do you think?"

"I don't know. How should I know? I can't open my eyes." She spoke toward the ceiling, Ernie's lips still against her neck.

"We really run into some lulus, don't we?" the driver said.

"What do you mean?"

"Nothing. Just talking to keep awake. That's what you want, isn't it?"

"What were you getting at, though?"

"I'm not getting at anything. I just meant there's really some dillies around if you know where to look. I mean where do they get this stuff? My kid brother delivers laundry. You think he's proud of that? But he puts in an honest day's work and doesn't ask for any favors. Nobody gives him any handouts. And you can be damn sure I never got any either."

"Me neither," murmured Noreen.

"Oh, come off it. You've had your little fanny pampered since the day you were born."

"When was I ever pampered?"

"Don't make me sick. This wasn't my idea. You're the one wanted to pick him up. It's just that kind of attitude I don't like. I mean my brother works for a laundry, that's all I mean."

Ernie sensed that things were taking a wrong turn.

"Well, don't be mad at me," said Noreen.

"Oh, no, of course not."

"I haven't done anything."

"That's just what I mean. It's just that manipulative attitude."

"What attitude?"

"You're a couple of real winners. I mean we don't hoard what we have. Room in the car—fine. But then to sit right back and give us this crap while my brother has to deliver laundry, well, it just makes you wonder. When people want to get somewhere they take the bus. They don't ask somebody for a handout."

"I didn't ask you to stop," Ernie said, moving his head away from Noreen's. "You could of gone on by easy enough."

"No, I don't like it. My brother drives a laundry truck, but he pays his way."

"So?"

"So? So you think that's much of a job? Think he likes that? You think that's the kind of work he wants?" She was leaning forward, shouting now, and Noreen, her eyes still closed, screamed upward: "Stop it!"

"That's it. That does it," said the driver, applying the brakes, the car wobbling, veering, then bumping over the shoulder. "Now you've upset her. This is where we part company, buster. You're going to have to get along by yourself from here on. This just isn't going to work."

Ernie did not speak for a moment of bewildered humiliation, feeling as if he had done something terribly wrong, then as if he were being persecuted without reason, then wondering if perhaps the driver were joking. "Are you kidding me? You're crazy if you think I'm getting out here in the middle of the goddamn desert. Nobody'd ever pick me up out here."

"You'll make out. I don't have any worries about you."

"What's the matter, aren't I your type or something?"

"Oh, boy, that's a good one. That's really smart. You're just no end of laughs. So what are you waiting for?"

"I'm not getting out of this car." He looked to Noreen, but her eyes were closed and her face indicated nothing.

"Come on, don't get funny," said the driver.

"I'm not moving."

"I said I want you out of here."

"I don't care what you want. I'd be out here all night. What'd you pick me up for? Just to throw me out?"

"Get out!" screamed Noreen, her eyes still closed.

In the shock of betrayal, Ernie threw open the door. Outside in the cool air he wrenched open the back door and took his canvas bag from among the packs and sleeping bags.

"No hard feelings," said the driver, her face sallow in the dim overhead light. "We're glad to help a guy out, but this was just getting too crowded."

Noreen had not moved. Ernie cursed and slammed the door, returning the women to darkness. The rear wheels spun on the gravel, he kicked the fender, ran and kicked it again, and was left behind. The taillights diminished until finally there was not a light anywhere in sight, except the stars, and they were numberless and incredibly remote. An uneasy realization of his solitude came over Ernie. There was not a sound anywhere; several times he looked behind him to dispel a sense of abysmal blackness at his back. At last a pair of headlights appeared. As they drew closer, the sense of isolation decreased and he imagined himself riding on again. Moving farther onto the highway, he put out his arm. The car came up in a blaze of light, swerved out and sped on. Ernie wandered short distances and stood with his weight on one leg and then the other. At intervals a car raced by.

Convinced it was hopeless, he crossed the highway to where the ground was higher. For a considerable distance he tramped through sparse brush, until he felt he could not be seen by passing motorists. In that enormous silence he felt unsafe. The only sound was a breeze rustling sporadically over the ground. He lay down, and with his head resting on his bag, the earth yawing under him as he looked at the immense sweep of the stars, he waited for dawn.

He was wakened by a terrific thundering he knew instantly was a train, and he leaped up in terror, certain he had fallen asleep on a railroad track. The train passed him at twenty yards, hissing and clattering, its great light rolling like an eye, the first cars rushing by before he realized he had never been in their path. With a pounding heart he watched the curtained Pullmans hurtling by. The dining car passed with Negroes in white garments working in the lighted kitchen. No one appeared to notice him. Then the train was gone, a rumble and a single red light fading rapidly away in the nebulous distance. The sky was the color of slate. Far away the beams of a car wavered in the lightening air.

Ernie walked back through the brush to the road, anxious to get home to Faye and filled again with resentment at being left here. In the increasing light his abandonment took on the unreality of something distant and inexplicable, though it could not have been longer than two or three hours ago that he had been put out of the car. Maybe, he thought, it had been the driver who had been attracted to him all along. But he still despised her, and he remembered Noreen with a pang of disappointment. All he was sure of was that he had been dealt a colossal insult. Lonely by the side of the road, he reviewed his bout, and it too had lost some of its vividness, though its import seemed as great as before: he was on his way.

Ernie was picked up at sunrise by a soldier in civilian clothes with sport shirts of all colors hanging from a metal rod across the entire width of the back seat, who owned two cars, had made love to innumerable women, drove at high speeds and talked with few pauses across Nevada and all the way to Sacramento. There the two parted. Ernie went the last forty-five miles by Greyhound, riding through the night coolness of low delta fields, past dark vineyards, orchards and walnut groves, isolated lights of farm houses, irrigation ditches full of moonlit water, then on the outskirts a gigantic technicolor face speaking silently on the screen of a drive-in movie. Dazed with fatigue yet alert in the eagerness of coming home, he rode into the city. The bus passed block after block of dark and dimly-lit houses. It stopped; the door opened and shut, then the bus bumped over railroad tracks and entered the downtown business district, the stores dark, box offices closed at the theaters, the marquee lights off, cars cruising down Main Street, and the empty sidewalks brightly lit. Ernie rose, and when the bus roared into the depot he was standing at the head of the aisle. He came lightly down the metal steps into balmy air and diesel fumes, and feeling in himself the potent allegiance of fate, he pushed open the door to the lobby, where unkempt sleepers slumped upright on the benches.

OTHER NEW YORK REVIEW CLASSICS

For a complete list of titles, visit www.nyrb.com.